HALLYU

MARTIN PETERSEN

HALLYU

Volume two

East Asian popular culture in a transnational perspective

A National Museum of Denmark Collection

University Press of Southern Denmark 2022

University of Southern Denmark Studies in History and Social Sciences Vol. 630
Layout and cover: Dorthe Møller, Unisats
Cover: "Thunder". Artist: Pernille Højfeld Nielsen
Printed by Narayana Press

ISBN 978-87-408-3395-9

Hallyu is published with support from
Academy of Korean Studies
Farumgaard-Fonden
Korea Foundation
Kulturministeriets Forskningspulje
National Museum of Denmark
Toyota-Fonden

University Press of Southern Denmark
55 Campusvej
DK-5230 Odense M
www.universitypress.dk

Distribution in the United States and Canada:
Independent Publishers Group
814 Franklin Street
Chicago, Il 60610
USA
www.ipgbook.com

Distribution in the United Kingdom:
Gazelle
White Cross Mills
Hightown
Lancaster
LA1 4 XS
U.K.
www.gazellebookservices.co.uk

Contents

Dor
Bitten

Camilla

Introduction

A day in the life of a Danish fan of Korean popular culture: Two ethnographic sketches

Spring 1993. 19 years old, I was notified of being selected to a one-year youth exchange program in the Republic of Korea. Korea was the fifth choice on my list. I was the only Dane who applied for Korea that year, I was told by the international youth exchange organization in explanation. 3rd year high school student, I knew almost nothing about the country. I remembered broadcast images of student demonstrations in Seoul, occasional coverage of the North-South conflict and something about Christian fervour. I knew that many Korean children were adopted to Denmark. I found a book in Danish on Korea and a few records labelled under the 'Folk music' category in the local library. I met the person who had been on exchange in a previous year. He talked about losing his calm in public transportation due to a feeling of utter alienation. And off I went.

Spring 2014. Anne shows up for the interview session with a parasol. She is in her last year of high school.[1] "The stuff that's not Korea – that's school. All the time that's left, I spend on Korea," she says. Anne watches the same Korean TV-drama episodes twice. First time, it is for enjoyment. Second time, she watches it without subtitles, trying to pick up phrases and vocabulary.

Her interest in Korea started in 2011 when she was fifteen. She first discovered the music when she was a member of a manga fan-club who met

1 All informants have been anonymized.

on afternoons. She refers to the music as K-pop. K-pop is an abbreviation of Korean pop. This 'K' frames, highlights and promotes selected aspects of Korean culture as a distinct national entity, as consumer products and fan items. After discovering K-pop sounds and visuals came an ever broadening interest in Korean language, history and culture.

K-pop, K-drama, K-food, K-fashion... These 'K's transgress the national borders and arrive globally under the umbrella term 'Hallyu'. The Korean Wave is created by creative industries and supported by the Korean state as a key soft power component, which soaks the global consumer in culture and products.

A day in the life of Anne anno 2014 is usually spent keeping up with the K-pop scene, K-drama and K-fashion through Danish and international Facebook groups and web portals. Anne reads and watches what other fans, bloggers and professional writers share and post in these mainly English language, online communities. She practices singing on her own with aid from MVs found on Youtube; here, she also finds variety shows, documentaries on social issues in South Korean society and on the North-South conflict. She writes a blog in Korean – guided by her Korean tutor, who is located in California. She frequently chats with Korean friends on KakaoTalk - a free mobile instant messaging application for smartphones widely used in Korea and Korea-oriented communities. Some are friends she met during a summer trip to Korea the previous year. At an Asian party in Copenhagen she got to know some Korean exchange students and youths living in Denmark – the number of especially young Korean on working holiday visas is slightly on the rise.[2] Anne occasionally also meets up with other Danish fans. They drink bubble tea (a product originating from Taiwan and globally associated with

2 From 2011 to 2014 there was a slight rise in the number of Korean individuals in Denmark on a working holiday visa. 2011: 36, 2012: 68, 2013: 60, 2014: 79. Source: http://whic.mofa.go.kr/contents.do?contentsNo=4&menuNo=6

Asian diaspora and Asia related fandoms) and occasionally go to meet-ups in parks. Here, they talk about K-pop and issues related to their shared fandom. Anne is fascinated by the Korean concept of cuteness (*aegyo*). Cuteness, she explains, is in the manner of speaking for instance. To her, cuteness is more appealing than sexy style. Anne especially dresses up in cute style for meet-ups, conventions and parties. In everyday life she strives to present herself with big eyes, a small mouth and white skin, like her Hallyu idols. The parasol she carries along to be able to protect her pale complexion. She got the inspiration from K-dramas. In Seoul, however, she mainly saw mature women ('aunts') doing this. She laughs.

This is an excerpt of a narrative related by a young, Danish female fan of Korean popular culture during an interview session in 2014 – juxtaposed to glimpses of my own discovery of Korea some twenty years earlier. I do not claim any particular representativeness with this small portrait. The significance of social media and websites, on- and off-line local and global communities combined with a broad palette of preferences for sounds, aesthetics, narratives and beauty ideals, however, are all features that indicate the level and degree of intimacy with Korean popular culture experienced by Anne. This intimacy is significantly present in the stories and narratives by the Danish informants, which are found throughout this book.

At its core, this book attempts to arrive at an understanding of and give a presentation of the intimacy as it is lived and experienced by Anne and her fellow fans of the various 'K's – more than anything K-pop and the range of other Ks, media, formats and genres that K-pop stars spill into. The book is based on field study conducted in 2014-8 and qualitative interviews with a main focus on nine female Danish fans of Korean popular culture predominantly in their early 20s mainly in 2014-2016. K-pop, Hallyu and the fandom around it, globally and in Denmark, is ever evolving. To a Danish fan, who has entered this fan universe around the time of the publication of this volume (2022), the sense of change when reading about Anne and the Danish K-pop community in the mid-2010s may possibly be almost as acute as my own '1993 perspective' on it. This volume is an attempt to capture the Danish K-pop community in the mid-2010s and present it to the readers.

Contents

This volume is divided into two main parts. The first part presents the research in a longer chapter. Additionally, it introduces Hallyu in a Danish context through lengthy quotes from the main informants of the story. Also, Part One puts Danish Hallyu fandom in a regional fan and industry perspective. The second part catalogues fan productivity. It features fan creations and interviews with the Danish fans.

The volume is richly illustrated; images include documentary photos of a K-pop event at the National Museum of Denmark, fan meet-up photos taken by the fans themselves, reproductions of fan art and of other creative productions. Notably, the volume also features artworks and illustrations made by eleven artists and illustrators based in Denmark. These illustrations are made with inspiration from selected sequences of the volume.

Part One: Danish Hallyu Fans consists of three sections.

The first section is a research article. *Korean Dreams and K-pop Realities: Towards a typology of productive fans of Hallyu in Denmark* examines the emergence of Danish youth who, in varying degrees of intensity and by dissimilar means, identify with and belong to the loose cultural geography of Korea and East Asia. They aspire to integrate into the Korean social fabric through career choice, they produce K-pop realities by performing Korean dance, conforming to Korean aesthetics or beauty ideals, thinking through Korean story-worlds and finding viable alternatives to Danish youth sociality.

The analysis is mainly based on fieldwork conducted in 2014-16 and qualitative interviews with a main focus on nine female Danish fans of Korean popular culture predominantly in their early 20s. Departing from Iwabuchi Koichi 's notion of 'inter-Asian mediated referencing', the study shows how the mediated encounter through the consumption of in particular popular music but also various screen formats offers Danish fans a wider repertoire for reflecting on their own lives and societies in the light of East Asian modernities. In short, I argue that by examining Danish productive fans and their K-pop reality as trans-Asian mediated referencing we may find ways to go further beyond the conception of "Asia" as a region.

The second section, *Korean Dreams and K-pop Realities: A supplement* features ten quotes and interview excerpts. Each text elaborates on passages in *Korean Dreams and K-pop Realities* marked with [#]. This supplement thus aims to enlighten the reader further about the matter from the fans' own perspectives and observations.

In the third section, Danish Hallyu fandom is put into perspective through portraits of two K-pop industry professionals and a group of Hungarian K-pop fans.

Part Two: *Collection Catalogue* explores creations and media products made by Danish Hallyu fans. The National Museum of Denmark has put focus on East Asian popular culture in a transnational perspective in a number of exhibitions (*Girl with Parasol* (2013), *Cosplayer!* (2015-)) and events (*Hallyu* (2012), *Cosplay* (2014), *K-Day* (2015), *Cosplay NatNight* (2015), *East Asia NatNight* (2016), but the museum also has made an object and media collection. This collection will stay in the museum storage and archives for centuries to come and be available for further research and exhibitions. The collection catalogue combines object photographs and photographic documentation of the media products and their creation processes with stories told by the productive fans. 'Fan

accessories' presents a self-made deck of cards as an example of things that fans make which becomes part of their everyday lives. 'Fan fiction' includes excerpts from three stories and a narrative about the making of fan fiction. 'Cover dance' documents a fan-made music video and the different stages of making it. Lastly, 'Fan art' presents examples of how K-pop stars are rendered in art by fans.

East Asian popular culture in a transnational perspective series

Hallyu is the second publication in the four volume series *East Asian popular culture in a transnational perspective: A National Museum of Denmark Collection*. This series explores issues linked to the consumption and appropriation of East Asian popular culture in a Danish context and asks what this can contribute to our understanding of cultural flows in an East/West perspective.

Volume One: Cosplay deals with a community of Danish fans of Japanese popular culture whose fandom makes them distinctly identifiable as productive fans; namely fans who *appropriate* characters, story-worlds and design from manga, anime and video games and who *produce* cosplay. It is argued that the Danish cosplayers constitute a confident, vibrant community, which sees itself in the midst of actualizing manga and Japanese media worlds against the backdrop of childhood and early youth literacies and intimacies. This 'actualization' and its productivity is largely disconnected from Japanese cosplay communities and Japan beyond the point of media culture. Further, the convergence of something identified as distinctively Japanese with something in which 'nationality' does not matter is a central part of the link between manga, anime and video games from Japan and cosplayer productivity in Denmark.

Volume Two: Hallyu deals with Danish fans of Korean popular culture. As consumers of Korean popular culture, not least K-pop (Korean pop music), these fans aspire to integrate into the Korean social fabric through career choice; they produce 'K-pop realities' by performing Korean dance, conforming to Korean aesthetics or beauty ideals, thinking through Korean story-worlds and finding viable alternatives to Danish youth sociality. This constitutes an example of how East Asian popular culture is present in the formation of Danish youth culture in the 2010s.

Volume Three: Purikura explores how an ethnographic exhibition in a Danish setting can enable playful productivity around East Asian popular culture and, by extension, how this can become a step towards new ethnographic research and explorations. The book argues that mimetic empathy is one way to create understanding of and engagement in the ethnographic matter for visitors. The argument is based on a study of contemporary Japanese photo-booth photography (*purikura*) in its Japanese context and in the context of the National Museum of Denmark exhibition *Girl with Parasol – Japan in the Photo Studio* (2013-2014).

Volume Four: Museum Manhwa explores creativity at the interphase between cultural heritage institutions and creative industries. In 2019-2020, the National Museum of Denmark collaborated with four South Korean creators of comics and graphic art on themes related to Korea and Denmark. Choi Ho Chul, Ancco, Super Pink and Wooh Nayoung explored the Korean Collection in the National Museum of Denmark as well as themes related to Denmark historically and today. The volume presents the resulting comics and graphic works and their creation process in a 'museum fiction' and 'explorer' perspective. On this basis, *Museum Manhwa* examines in which ways objects, collections, narratives and expertise of museums and cultural heritage institutions can become a resource for creative industries in their work with narratives, characters, story-worlds, design, and aesthetics and how these creative collaborations can become integrated into the cultural heritage institutions, resulting in new types of content, work formats and visitor/user experiences.

In this manner, *Cosplay* (vol.1) and *Hallyu* (vol.2) focus on Danish productive fans. They engage theories on 'Asia as method', 'inter-Asian mediated referencing' and 'Asian sensibilities' as the frame for an inquiry into transnational relations between East Asian and Denmark around flows of popular culture from the perspective of Danish 'productive fans'.

Meanwhile, *Purikura* (vol.3) and *Museum Manhwa* (vol.4) focus on the museum institution in a transnational perspective. They explore creativity and develop notions of playful productivity and museum fiction in a Danish cultural heritage and museum institution perspective.

The 'East Asian Popular Culture in a Transnational Perspective' series and the current volume on Danish Hallyu fans have been made with the academic as well as the general reader in mind. The general reader may find an easily accessible and extensive introduction to Hallyu and its Danish fans in Part Two.

I approach the topic from perspectives and fields such as fan studies, Korean and East Asian studies and cultural studies. I strive to introduce relevant discourses and key terminologies in the research chapter in Part One in a manner which is accommodative towards students and scholars arriving from these various disciplines. While scholarly readers may only read the research chapter, the other sections will hopefully also be of value. Not only does Part Two extensively present empirical findings, it may also inspire other scholarly approaches, as well as provide a broad insight into Hallyu fandom in Denmark. In short, it is my hope that this book will serve its dual purpose as research publication and museum catalogue for the general and the scholarly reader alike.

Acknowledgements

First and foremost, I would like to thank the fans of Korean popular culture who have kindly and with enthusiasm shared their interests, life-worlds and insights with me. In many cases, they did so in several interview sessions over a time span of several years. I would also like to thank them deeply for allowing me to publish their fan art, photos, excerpts of their fan fiction and other creative productions in this volume and, to collect some of it for the National Museum of Denmark.

In the same breath, I would also like to thank the K-pop industry professionals who took time to present me with their perspectives on the topic.

A cornerstone in the *East Asian Popular Culture in a Transnational Perspective* series is the National Museum of Denmark. It has been a space for collaborative events and exhibitions with Danish fans of East Asian popular culture. Several colleagues at the museum have been important in this regard. Rikke Tjørnehøj has been an awesome work partner for most of these activities, always energetic, optimistic and supportive. Much the same words characterize Julie Emilie Stockholm Kragh and David Nicolas Christensen who have also been engaged in these museum events and contributed immensely to developing ideas and connections. Christian Sune Pedersen has provided organizational support.

Anna Frandsen, during her internship in the museum, made preliminary language revision and translation of parts of the volume and made several valuable comments.

Martin Lindø Westergaard and Dorthe Møller with University Press of Southern Denmark have been excellent collabration partners in the production of this book.

Andrew Jackson was helpful in the early development of the research chapter. Also, conversations with Nanna Holdgaard has influenced my perspective.

Lastly, I would like to thank one by one the illustrators and artists who received text excepts and background materials and produced the brilliant illustrations featured in this book. The established artists Trine Laier and Pernille Ørum have produced distinct expressions of Danish K-pop fandom. Johanna Aresvik, Maria Azevedo, Thit Bitsch, Emilie Højland, Matilde Landi, Ymir O'Neill, Sarah Santangelo, Astrid Stefánsdóttir and Sarah Thomas are students at The Animation Workshop in Viborg, Denmark. I immediately fell for their visions of Danish Hallyu fandom. Much to my delight I soon realized that many of them were, in fact, themselves fans of K-pop and tuned into Korean popular culture.

Early stages of research for this book was enabled by a one-year grant from Kulturministeriets Forskningspulje. The publication has been generously funded by Academy of Korean Studies (AKS-2019-P-11), the Farumgaard-Fonden, Toyota Fonden and the National Museum of Denmark. Generous funding from Korea Foundation has enabled collaboration with the Danish artists. Thank you!

Last, but not least, I would like to thank my family and loved ones for their support and inspiration.

Part One: Danish Hallyu Fans

Korean Dreams and K-pop Realities: Towards a typology of productive fans of Hallyu in Denmark

Introduction

This chapter aims to critically examine what the study of consumption and appropriation of Korean popular culture in a non-regional (in this case Danish) context can contribute to our understanding of cultural flows and trajectories of modernity from an East/West perspective. The chapter engages theories on 'Asia as method' and 'inter-Asian mediated referencing' as a frame of inquiry into transnational relations between Korea and Denmark that centre around flows of popular culture, as seen from the perspective of Danish 'productive fans'. The findings are based on qualitative interviews and a field study conducted mainly in 2014-6 focusing on nine Danish fans predominantly in their early 20s. I have mainly explored this productivity as formative of K-pop reality. In doing so, the chapter further aims to question previous studies of consumption and appropriation of Korean popular culture in US and European contexts, which often engage notions of orientalism and post-colonial critique.

Accordingly, this chapter addresses how the consumption and appropriation of Korean popular culture is formative of Danish youths as productive fans, to what extent this productivity has a transformative potential for Danish/East Asian relations and whether it is possible to reassess hitherto dominant understandings of globalization on the East/West axis.

Inter-Asian referencing[3]

In the field of cultural studies – which examines intra-regional flows of culture – it has been argued that East Asia, in its linear trajectory of capitalist consumerist modernity (Chua 2008), is more than a historical condition; it is also to a great extent constituted and transformed by a trans-Asian public. This cultural geography is shaped by national and commercial interests, formed under the influence of Western modernity and structural appropriation of principally American media systems in regional centres such as Hong Kong, Japan and South Korea (Iwabuchi 2002; Chua 2012; Condry 2006). It is, however, also shaped by consumers, fans and grassroots communities, who establish affective communities of imaginative 'prosumers'

---

3 In *Cosplay* (Vol. 1), I examine these same issues from the perspective of Japanese popular culture. This section is similar to a section in the research chapter in *Cosplay*.

(producer-consumers) and 'approreaders' (appropriator-readers) (Iwabuchi 2010: 87). These terms constitute a focus on consumers as participants who not only passively receive and are ideologically formed by messages, but who, by the reception of cultural texts, are appropriative and productive in a sense that is often in contrast to dominant meanings.[4] This descriptive terminology is imbued with progressive aspirations, which often contradict the commercial aspects of popular culture. A wide range of research has focused on trans-cultural pop cosmopolitans (Jung 2011), who constitute themselves in on/offline communities in the East Asian region with interests in, for example, Hong Kong cinema (Chua 2012), manga, anime and video games from Japan (Iwabuchi 2002) and South Korean TV-dramas and pop music (Chua & Iwabuchi 2008; Kim 2013). These studies have justifiably complicated the understanding of globalization as predominantly unfolding on a 'West to East' axis.

A key movement in this field is the advocacy for regional re-orientation, termed 'Asia as method' (Chen 2010). Chen Kuan-Hsing argues that the notion of Asia may be used as an imaginary anchor point, and that Asian societies can become one another's point of reference so that the understanding of self can be transformed and subjectivity rebuilt through 'decolonization, deimperialization, and de cold War' (ibid.: 212). In this manner, claims Chen, the method can potentially accentuate alternative understandings of world history. Ultimately, Chen's project signifies a radical re-writing of the global order and may be seen as a move towards pan-Asianism.[5] Engaging 'Asia as method'[6] with reference to affective communities of intra-regional, transnational pop cosmopolitans, Iwabuchi is a bit more cautious when he highlights

4 An early, significant example of this frame in fan studies is Henry Jenkins' elaboration on 'textual poachers' (1992).

5 Importantly, Chen does not use this term himself in *Asia as Method*.

6 Iwabuchi also uses the term '(pop)Asia as method' in a 2012 Nippop seminar presentation in Bologna. https://www.youtube.com/watch?v=CkAo20raASs

a shift from 'mediated inter-Asian referencing' towards mutual collaboration at grassroots level in the East Asian region.[7] Iwabuchi has elaborated on this notion over a range of papers (2010, 2010a, 2013, 2014, 2015) and explains mediated inter-Asian referencing as follows:

> People in Asian countries have long tended to face the West to interpret their own modern experiences, but the mediated encounter with other Asian modernities through the consumption of TV dramas, film and popular music from other parts of the region now offers people a wider repertoire for reflecting on their own lives and societies in the light of other East Asian modernities (2014: 51).

Modern East Asia should be understood here as a 'loose cultural geography' (ibid: 48) imbued with regional cultural proximity and resonance, and the inter-Asian referencing as 'an integral part of people's mundane experiences of consuming media cultures' (ibid: 51). Here, Iwabuchi shares common ground with Cho Young Han, who argues that the consumption of pan-Asian pop cultures is limited to but not determined by this topography. It enables East Asian sensibilities which "[f]ollowing Williams's insight [...] can be interpreted as emerging structures of feeling within the cultural geography of the region that encompass 'meanings and values as they are actively lived and felt' as well as 'a social experience which is still in process, often indeed not yet recognized as social but taken to be private, idiosyncratic, and even isolating' " (p. 132) (Cho 2011: 393).

Iwabuchi does not preclude mediated inter-Asian referencing from social spaces beyond the loose cultural geography of East Asia. Notably, he

7 Iwabuchi also uses the term to imply what should be expected of researchers in terms of academic theoretisation (Iwabuchi, 2014, 48). My use of the term in this chapter does not have such implications.

has suggested that '[t]he inclusion of Asian migrants living in Western countries in trans-Asian cultural connection would be imperative to go beyond a closed conception of "Asia" as a region (2015: 7). Here, I am interested in seeing if we can push the boundaries of this concept of mediated referencing even further. I explore this aspect from the perspective of the Western fan immersed in the consumption of Korean popular culture, and use the term 'trans-Asian mediated referencing', which should then also include non-Asian productive fans. Iwabuchi (and other researchers with him) sometimes employ the terms 'inter-Asian' and 'trans-Asian' as interchangeably referring to the Asian region, although the term 'trans-Asian' may also refer to Asian (im) migrants living beyond the region. What I explore here is thus the notion of mediated referencing, in which the term 'trans-Asian' refers to social spaces and people beyond both regional and ethnic perspectives who are instead delimited by a sense of shared-ness and cultural connection around East Asian popular and media cultures. Preliminarily, I outline the ways in which studies of Asian (im)migrant consumption of Hallyu and some previous studies on the Western fan of East Asian popular culture deal with these issues.

Migrants, fans and cultural critique

Various studies have treated Asian migrant consumption of East Asian popular cultural in Europe and the US. In *The Korean Wave: Korean Media Go Global*, editor Kim Youna 'argues for the Korean Wave's double capacity in the creation of new and complex spaces of identity that are both enabling and disenabling cultural diversity in a digital cosmopolitan world' (2013: 3). Throughout the present volume, Hallyu is examined both in the 'context of transnational migration systems and processes' (ibid: 87) and often concurrently, although to a lesser degree, from the perspective of non-Asian Western fans and observers.

Based on an ethnographic case study in Austria, Sung Sang-Yeon in the chapter "Digitization and online cultures of the Korean Wave" argues that East Asian (im)migrants[8] in Europe 'construct a strong pan-Asian community by consuming Korean popular culture' (2013: 135). According to Sung, 'Korean popular culture contains "Asian values" more than other Asian products' (ibid: 138). This gives East Asian (im)migrants a sense of being Asian. Such a sense of community should be seen in the context of a feeling of marginalization and distance felt in Austria (ibid: 146). While this chapter only passingly concerns itself with non-(im)migrant perspectives, Sung does note that 'East Asia and East Asian culture is not a central interest to many Austrians, who lack sufficient knowledge and information to appreciate it' (ibid: 139). With Sung, we thus gain an understanding of Korean popular culture in a European context, where it is predominantly configured in the context of (im)migrant perspectives and in contrast to mainstream society.

Park Jung-Sun in "Negotiating identity and power", a study which draws 'on ethnographic accounts of Korean youths' consumption of South Korean popular culture' in Los Angeles and Chicago (2013: 121), provides a more complex sense of the cultural flows between Korean (im)migrant youths, other Asian-American communities, the Korean cultural industry and non-Asian Americans. However, Park's focus on Korean popular culture in urban communities in the US is also significantly related to a sense of marginalization, contributing to a sense of home, entitlement and emotional comfort in (im)migrant youth communities (ibid: 127).

Beyond the Kim Youna edited volume, Tobias Hübinette in "The Reception and Consumption of Hallyu in Sweden: Preliminary Findings and Reflections", the first outline of the social constitution of Hallyu fandom in Scan-

8 My use of the term (im)migrant is not universally used in the texts I refer to. For consistency, I use the term throughout here.

dinavia, also emphasizes the (im)migrant perspective. 'Many if not most fans of K-pop are non-white working-class and often belong to the so-called 2nd generation, children of usually non-Western migrants, who live in segregated and underprivileged areas and suburbs dominated by a non-white population in the bigger and middle-sized cities of Sweden' (2012: 519).

Hübinette does, however, also identify educated white middle-class and working-class consumers. Beyond the perspective of class and ethnicity, he notes a predominance of young female fans of K-pop, 'a small principally white and male dominated middle- and upper-class based subculture' (ibid: 515) of Korean cinema, as well as 'a slight overrepresentation' of the LGBTQ community. In mainstream society, Hübinette mentions the marked presence of 'gook humour', according to which Asians in general are 'considered to look funny and ugly, and Asian women are associated with prostitution and international marriage, while Asian men are linked to everything that is not considered masculine thereby being both emasculated and infantilized' (ibid: 512).

In *Korean masculinities and transnational consumption* (2011), Jung Sun raises another noteworthy critique. On the basis of a transnational media/ethnographic consumer study of three localizations of popular culture representations of Korean masculinity in Japan (TV dramas), Singapore (pop music) and the West (film), she argues that, while the Japanese and Singaporean cases, may be characterized as post-colonialism and trans-pop consumerism respectively, Western online cult fandom around the 'Asian extreme' film *Oldboy* is characterized by post-Orientalism. This reading is mainly based empirically on Western cult fandom as observed through user comments and film reviews on English-language-based film websites such as the following:

> Before [I started watching recent South Korean films], my knowledge about Korea was very limited. One is M*A*S*H, in which the Korean War seems to never end. Then, some photos of [South] Korean students protesting during the 80s ... [and] of North Korean people in extreme poverty ... [but] Dae-Soo is totally cool ... totally savage but cool ... like Alex from *Clockwork Orange.*
>
> *– Gu, 39, an Australian fan of South Korean films from Melbourne (Jung 2011: 119)*

Jung concludes that the 'transgressive machinic South Korean masculinity becomes the West's techno-Orientalist fantasy' (ibid: loc.3622). In "K-pop female idols in the West", Jung Eun-Young descibes how racialized, hyper-feminized performatives of K-pop girl bands like Wonder Girls and Girl Generation play to Western stereotypes. Jung's observations of the US consumers and media users are, as with Jung Sun, partly substantiated through somewhat idiosyncratic readings of user comments on YouTube and Twitter. On this basis, Jung notes a binary of cultural critique on the one hand and 'stereotypical notions of Asian-ness in their racial and sexual identities' (2013: 117) on the other. The latter imagined stereotypes, Jung infers, 'have proven to be remarkably resistant to change as manifest in the responses to Asians by young and old Americans alike' (ibid: 117). Interestingly though, Jung does not engage with the critical or more balanced positions, with the result that non-Asian/non-Korean US viewers and audiences seem to be subsumed as Westerners who hold eroticized images and imagined desires for racially Asian females (ibid: 109). While such appropriations are observable and documented, in these researches the non-(im)migrant mainly references notions of Western cultural hegemony and mainstream society, white majority culture and the anonymous internet commentary.

Leaving aside (im)migrant perspectives, previous studies of consumption and appropriation of East Asian popular culture in US and European contexts have also questioned the transformative potential inherent in these 'East to West' cultural flows. Henry Jenkins' seminal fan studies (1992; 2006) disentangled the fan from dominant mainstream understandings as stigmatized, socially reclusive, abnormal, in excess or even perverted, and he launched the fan as a central figure for understanding the concept of identity formation in current participatory media cultures. Jenkins demonstrates how the top-down structure of media industries and nation states intersect with fans, who appropriate and participate in popular culture in a wide range of ways, thus giving shape to a convergence culture, a culture which is increasingly characteristic of late modern, highly technological societies (Jenkins, Ford & Green 2013). Despite this, Jenkins claims that the 'pop cosmopolitan walks a thin line between dilettantism and connoisseurship, between orientalistic fantasies and a desire to honestly connect with and understand an alien culture ... ' (2006: 164).

My ambition here is thus to assess transformative practices in a demarcated locality and through this critically engage the above-mentioned studies of trans-Asian popular culture and Hallyu appropriations in non-Asian, non-(im)migrant and, for that matter, non-mainstream society contexts.

Methodology

The study is mainly based on fieldwork that took place between February 2014 and February 2016. It deals with a community of Danish fans of South Korean popular culture whose fandom make them visible and discernible as prosumers; fans who *consume* pop music, TV dramas and entertainment and *produce* fan fiction, cover dance, fan-sites and themselves.

The fieldwork has mainly been structured around semi-structured, qualitative interviews with these productive fans. As well as a combination of solo and small group interviews, the fieldwork was also conducted online and in the museum setting[9] in which most of the informants were constituted as co-organizers, participants and presenters in the National Museum of Denmark event, *K-Day*.[10] I have also studied Facebook groups and sites such as Danish ELFs[11] and *Danish K-pop loverš!!* .[12]

I am interested here in outlining the typology of Danish fans and their productivity through individual voices and narratives. To bring out these voices and narratives in the context of the specificity of their 'fan productiveness', I have organized the remaining part of the chapter into sections which present nine Danish Hallyu fans. Here, the community is introduced through glimpses into the fandom of the nine informants. (The supplement (pp. 53-67) further elaborates informant perspectives through quotes. Each section references the relevant quotes with an #.) This way of outlining the Danish Hallyu community should also be seen as a way of reconsidering the notions of Western Hallyu consumers and observers, which surface in the writings outlined in the *Migrants, fans and cultural critique* section above.[13]

9 A central aspect of the participant-observations is thus that I activate a museum field. I developed the theoretical basis for this field approach in connection with my PhD dissertation and in later research in the format of methodological experiments with the East Asian collections in the National Museum of Denmark as my point of departure. See *Purikura* (vol. 3) and *Museum Manhwa* (vol. 4)

10 A group of Korean studies students and fans of Korean popular culture participated in the preparation for this event. http://natmus.dk/museerne/nationalmuseet/aktiviteter/k-day-sydkoreansk-popkultur-paa-nationalmuseet/ http://www.mynewsdesk.com/dk/nationalmuseet/pressreleases/den-sydkoreanske-boelge-rammer-nationalmuseet-1146714

11 Danish ELFs is a group for Danish fans of Super Junior

12 With its 1103 members (as of January 6, 2016) this community is a Facebook group dedicated to fans of all kinds of Korean music.

13 Apart from Hübinette, this research does not base its critique on qualitative interviews with, or fieldwork on, Western observers and fans of Hallyu.

Towards a typology of productive fans of Hallyu in Denmark

Bitten / reflexive euphoria

Bitten was the first informant I interviewed. I had sent a message to an administrator of the largest Danish K-pop fan community on Facebook, *Danish K-pop loverš!!*, who suggested I contact Bitten as she had "an extensive knowledge of K-pop and [...] does not have any particular prejudices against certain [K-pop] groups [...]".[14]

In our first interview session Bitten, administrator of the Danish Super Junior fan group and a student of Japanese studies, kindly informed me about Korea, K-pop, K-drama and Hallyu fandom in Denmark. It took me another session to fully realize and appreciate that this facilitating role, as also appreciated by the administrator, was Bitten's strength and the place where her contribution to fan productivity rests. Bitten is a fan who, through her eloquence and analytical perspective, helped bring out a sense of comprehensibility to Danish fan-girl perspectives on K-pop masculinities. This was to all appearances also the way that she conveyed and shared this reflexive consumer perspective as a fan-site administrator, in conversation with her friends and fellow fans in the community and in fan meet-ups in places like Kongens Have (King's Garden), which is a public park in central Copenhagen **[#1]**.

---

14 Unless otherwise note, all quotes from conversations with Danish informants have been translated from the Danish.

Fans of Korean popular culture, like Bitten, gain an understanding of the terrain through translations. They actively seek these translations, most concretely of the linguistic kind, through the media industry or fan-subbed TV-dramas, variety shows and translated K-pop lyrics. However, they also seek 'cultural translations' as in the case of the video blog *Eat Your Kimchi*, which has a key facilitating and gatekeeping role for many Danish fans. Korea is made partially comprehensible through these video blogs produced by a couple of Seoul-based Canadian teachers turned full-time bloggers. However, even in this vibrant transnational field, *Eat Your Kimchi* cannot be understood separately from the K-pop world. These bloggers inspire, cooperate and interact with artists and companies. Bitten has no personal interaction with the K-pop world, as the *Eat Your Kimchi* team does. Yet her status as mediator and cultural translator in the loosely organized Danish fan community is comparable.

As such, Bitten is arguably the type of fan who Kim Youna finds at the intersection of illusion and realism:

> K-pop performers exemplify a sort of pop perfectionism – catchy tunes, good singing, attractive bodies, cool clothes, mesmerizing movements, and other attractive attributes in a non-threatening, pleasant package (Lie 2012). This pleasurable experience can make international fans feel how difficult it is not to enjoy it, even when they may be fully aware of its addictiveness and extremely photogenic, visual illusion (2013: 9).

In a kind of reflexive pleasure, or critical euphoria, Bitten immerses herself in communal celebration of this pop perfectionism while simultaneously de-constructing it. She immerses herself in what I will refer to here as 'K-pop reality'. By this, I refer to a plethora of fan activities which arise from and extend the pleasure of pop perfectionism. In the case of Bitten, this includes making birthday cakes in celebration of K-pop performers, playing games with home-made playing cards featuring K-pop performers (See Part Two: Fan accessories pp. 75-80), teasingly debating biases (the fan's preferred artist) and treating K-pop performers as imaginary boyfriends, decorating walls and smart phone folders with photos, sharing fan service videos to name just a few of her activities that centre mainly around boybands such as Super Junior, ShiNEE, and EXO.

The deconstructive, critical and reflexive aspects of Bitten's fan productivity is expressed through identifying the formulaic, pinpointing the marketing strategy and considering the cynical promotion of Korean masculinities packaged in the mediated format of K-pop performers. Often, the shift between euphoria and critique would occur within the same segment of conversation as a kind of pendular shift – exemplified in the following quote where Bitten is comparing K-pop performers to a packaging and then elaborates:

> If you get a watch which is broken, you'll return it. It's a bit the same with them [the K-pop performers]. If there's a flaw in the packaging ... For example, EXO or some of the other groups ... How do they [the companies] find them? They are so perfect. The boy bands; their image typically is very, very perfect. Surely, they have flaws, and that's what many people like ... Even the human aspects are incredibly sweet ... It is enormously commercial that they are so perfect.

Certainly, Bitten is not one of the 'ignorant' Westerners described by Sung Sang-Yeon. Arguably, she straddles Jung Eun-Young's stereotyping/critiquing binary of social media commentators. Bitten is not cynical, but her position is firmly based on a realization of how the Korea she loves is somehow contained in the K-pop universe.

A significant case in point, Bitten remains attentive to the continuities and rifts between K-pop reality on one hand and Korean sociality on the other. She is aware of the ways in which Korean masculinities offer themselves as consumable via a range of practices, which to some of the informants in this study constitute a pleasurable alternative to Danish masculinity; not least when it comes to the perceived interplay between soft and hard masculinity (Jung 2011). This comes out most lucidly when Bitten talks about how K-pop performer fan services with perceived homosocial/erotic elements are understood by some Danish fangirls:

> Many people think that Korea is liberal because they have these TV-shows ... either they don't know it, or else they don't think about it, but if that really had been the case that they [the K-pop performers] were homosexual, then it hadn't been accepted [in Korea]. Many young Danish girls in Denmark like that they are open. 'Wow! He can really be feminine and wear girls' clothes' ... They just don't know that it is an act in a way.

This consumption and Bitten's resultant fan productivity cannot be reduced to an imperialist, white woman's gaze and the objectification of Asian male (machinic) bodies. It is, however, a highly mediated field in which Korean masculinity is identified from the outside as a kind of dreamscape shared by fans.

Much in line with her role as cultural translator and gatekeeper, Bitten introduced me to two of her friends, Camilla and Dora, whose fan productivity I will explore next.

Camilla / ubiquity and mind-writing

The majority of the fans I interviewed had come across K-pop and Hallyu via an initial interest in manga, anime and other aspects of Japanese popular culture **[#2]**. Bitten, as we have just seen, was a student of Japanese studies. Some fans told me that, after discovering and becoming engaged in Hallyu fandom, they had 'grown out of' their initial interest in manga and anime. Camilla, however, as a productive fan, engaged a dual interest in Japanese and Korean popular culture in order to create a hybrid world in her mind that exists somewhere between K-pop and anime; a genre of fan fiction in which anime characters are inserted into the K-pop universe, and where plot, mood, structure and characters are built up around the friendships and interrelations of the K-pop artists:

> With K-pop I actually have a story in my mind, with characters from an anime, of course, where they live as 'K-pop idols'. With K-pop I actually get a lot of inspiration from interviews and shows, where you experience their friendship and comradeship.

This is a world that exists only inside Camila's mind – a constructed dreamscape which is not written down in any form. The characters are based upon the Japanese anime *Beyblade*, which Camilla has been watching since she was a child. Meanwhile, the story follows the whole process from rookie to top idol in the K-pop universe. The result is a coming-of-age *bildungsroman* of sorts, based on numerous K-pop idols, their experiences, what they do and how they live.

In the case of Camilla, her K-pop reality is thus actualized via a creative, inner dialogue which unfolds in the borderland that lies between authorship, daydreaming and fantasy – a kind of fan fiction of the mind. Fan fiction, in its occasional appropriation of actual people in narratives, which at times engage

themes of sexuality, violence and angst among others, is regarded as transgressive by some fans and outside observers (Hellekson & Busse 2014). Camilla is a case in point. She finds it unethical to bring actual K-pop performers into her fictional universe, and she draws clear boundaries between fictional universes and non-fiction life-worlds. The flawlessly flawed, cute and beastly male K-pop performers are after all vulnerable and exposed human beings – a recurrent and somewhat ambiguously defined concern often raised by informants.

Camilla then puts these two distinct creative universes in her mind into words: '[...] this story, and many others, are in constant development, since I don't write them down, they can be constantly changed and expanded.' In all its privacy, immateriality and mutability, her mind-writing follows the literary and formal conventions of fan fiction. The internet, not least the *Asianfanfics* site, is abundant with fan fiction based on K-pop stars and *Beyblade* (and other Japanese popular culture narratives) respectively. Camilla had in fact read a few fan fiction stories, which, like her own, combined elements of K-pop and *Beyblade*. The originality of her work, however, is not of relevance here. What is important is the way productive fans effortlessly navigate between East Asian cultural formats and media universes as consumers and as productive fans (further on Camilla's mind writing, see Part Two: Fan fiction pp. 80-82).

Camilla's case thus helps expand and nuance the meaning of 'fan productivity'. The appropriation of East Asian formats and contents, in particular the engagement with Korean masculinities in K-pop reality, may or may not escape the scholarly critique of Western mainstream and fan discourse and the appropriations raised in *Migrants, fans and cultural critique*. However, as a form of productivity, and through the narrative power this has in Camilla's everyday life, her ubiquitous mind-writing insists that we should not stop our inquiry at the threshold of imagined desires for 'animated' Korean males, but consider the power and effect with which these images and life-worlds saturate the dreamscape of Danish fans. As such, Camilla's mind-writing is arguably a strong example of how East Asian media worlds flow into Danish life-worlds and consciousness to constitute a loose cultural geography which unfolds in K-pop reality with its biases (the fan's preferred artist), shipping (coupling of idols and characters in fandom) and pleasurable engagement with the 'cute flaws' and flawless sexualities of male K-pop performers.

Dora / mimetics

Camilla takes on the 'Korean dream' in a very literal manner with her creative reveries. Bitten navigated and laid out the Korean dreamscape in an organized yet playful manner, which helped delimit this loose cultural geography. In comparison, Dora's fan productivity and trans-Asian mediated referencing is more material and embodied in that it takes place through the physical (re)enactment of K-pop cover dancing. Dora frequently practices K-pop cover dance, has occasionally posted videos on her YouTube channel and has participated in a few cover dance contests as well. My interview sessions with Dora were associative rollercoaster rides through her K-pop reality. Our conversations often centred around and were infused by the familiar themes of flawlessly flawed Korean men, biases, shipping and fan service, liberally peppered with her spontaneous recital of K-pop lyrics. Dora embodied the fangirl.

As a cover dancer, her aim is to reproduce the dance in a manner that mimics the original as closely as possible. In this, Dora corresponds to most, but certainly not all, cover dancers. This bodily mimesis was also more subtly discernible in Dora's general stylistic observations (her choice of clothing style, beauty products, her nail art and so forth.) She has a changing understanding – if not to the point of actual emulation – of plastic surgery as well as other beauty ideals which are considered characteristic of Korea in Danish Hallyu fandom.

Dora in particular discovered Korea through her favourite K-pop boyband SHINee. She emphasizes a feeling of intimacy and admiration of the mental and physical discipline of these male K-pop performers, their perceived humanity and their good looks **[#3]**. While this more consumptive aspect of her fandom takes up the majority of her time, as compared to the time spent on practicing and performing cover dance, this consumption is interrelated with and amplifies the experience of the infectious K-pop beats, which Dora found irresistible to the point at which she felt she just had to dance. Dora at times regards her immersion in this kind of dream-world as excluding, in the sense that it is not easily communicable beyond the fandom community, and in the sense that the Hallyu fangirl and her passions – according to most fans I spoke with – are not held in high esteem in Danish mainstream youth society **[#4]**. Dora encounters a variety of comments on K-pop, to confirm that East Asian popular culture – at least in its K-pop form – is frequently regarded as silly, 'gooky', emasculated, gayish (in a negative sense), as noted by Jung (2013), Jung Sun (2011), Hübinette (2012) and Sung (2013).

The link between Dora's occasional experience of marginalization as a K-pop fan and her activities with cover dance should not be overstated, however. Likewise, the link between her specific affection for K-pop perfectionism as performed by SHINee and her dance routines can also easily be exaggerated. The referencing in her actual practice of cover dance is not specifically an embodiment of fan affection in those terms. Dora surely sometimes chooses a dance based on her affections for the male performers of SHINee, but she also recurrently chose dances by female K-pop performers, with whom she does not feel any particular bond, but whose *aegyo* style she seeks to emulate. A key term in the vocabulary of Danish Hallyu fans, Dora understands *aegyo* as referring to 'cuteness' but, as she adds, a certain kind of cuteness. Dora specifically associates *aegyo* with a Korean girl or young woman with big eyes, light make-up, bright or peach coloured lips and who looks innocent. Importantly, *aegyo* style is observable in both boy- and girl-band music videos where focus is on charming the viewer by drawing attention to facial expressions and flowing, often playful dance moves. Dora attains *aegyo* by embodying the above aspects and by 'trying to make it look like the dance is a game I am playing, and as something that is more natural, a part of me' (See Part Two: Cover dance pp. 94-99). In this bodily mimesis, in this actualization of K-pop reality, there is a clear sense of becoming, of somehow belonging within the Hallyu dreamscape.

By looking at Dora, Bitten and Camilla's cases, we can obtain a grasp of the way in which Asian modernity is perceived and experienced exactly as that; a kind of modernity that can be engaged with through imitation, critique, humour, distancing and intimacy. While, indeed, humour and distancing do sometimes combine in fan narratives, it is not a nicely compartmentalized, lower-hierarchy entity of past-ness, timelessness or exoticism used to distance oneself from by means of racial imagining, 'gook humour' and techno-Orientalist fantasies.

Gene and Helen / prescriptiveness, mimetics and counter-identities

When interviewing these and other female fans, I habitually asked about the presence of Danish male fans of Korean popular culture. Gene often came up in these conversations as a rare and prominent example. When I met him for an interview session, Gene brought along Helen.

Gene comes from an Asian migrant family background and Helen, with one migrant background parent, both fall outside the empirical scope of this chapter but their contribution is relevant from a comparative perspective. Gene was highly engaged in the K-pop universe and strongly oriented towards developing the Danish fan community. As an active participant in Danish conventions featuring Japanese popular culture, he said that he aspired to develop a similar community around Korean popular culture. This involved a desire to have Korean popular culture assume a more prominent position at these conventions, and to sustain offline K-pop communities through more frequent fan meet-ups (which at the time of the interview seemed, in fact, to be getting less frequent). His community orientation had an expressly prescriptive side. He once sparked an online debate and stirred feelings within K-pop fandom with a post that set out to define what constitutes a real fan.[15] If this prescriptiveness constitutes one part of his fan productivity (as was also the case for Bitten), then another part was predominantly mimetic (as with Dora). He identified with *ulzzang* aesthetics, which include using skin-whitening products and contact lenses, buying Asian clothes online and striving for the v-line **[#5]**.

To Gene, these practices came together in an aesthetic of flawlessness and perfection, which thus explicitly associates the K-pop universe with newness and modernity; a kind of ideal present. Actively pursuing this ethos of flawless masculinity made Gene stand out in the Danish fan community of Korean popular culture, in which boys and men are a minority, and also in mainstream Danish society, which in his own words and experience may perceive this kind of masculinity as gay or effeminate.

Helen admired Gene for his courage in performing *ulzzang* versions of masculinity, thereby defying perceived Danish stereotypes. She teasingly pinpointed his doubly marginalized yet confident positionality vis-à-vis both mainstream society and the fangirl-dominated Danish K-pop community. To Helen herself, being a fan of K-pop was connected to a preference for Asian males. This preference she framed outright as disinterest in Danish men and their version of masculinity. During my interviews with Danish fans of

15 A main point being that as a fan one should know and listen to several bands and be able to dance to at least so and-so many choruses.

East Asian popular culture, I encountered many narrations of marginalization, but Helen formulated the most outspoken rejection of Danish mainstream youth culture, viewing it as constituted according to American popular music with unrefined lyrics, and communities formed around parties, sex and alcohol **[#6]**. To her, the preferred lifestyle was attained through a long-distance relationship with a Southeast Asian male living in the US, making Asian friends online, listening to K-pop, drinking bubble tea with friends and practicing K-pop cover dance with Gene and a group of friends – associating herself in this manner with the loose cultural geography of Asia.

There is not sufficient basis for attributing these clearly stated senses of counter-identity to their (im)migrant backgrounds. I will note, however, that Gene and Helen's narratives resonate with the research of Sung (2013), Park (2013) and Hübinette (2012) above, and that the assertiveness found here as mimetic embodiment through *ulzzang* aesthetics, prescriptiveness and life-style ideology arguably was stated at its most emphatic by these two fans.

Ida / clear borders, blurred boundaries

I came across Ida in the Danish Super Junior fan group, which Bitten administered, when a friend posted a notification concerning a fan fiction she had posted on *Asianfanfics*. Compared to the other informants, particularly with regard to the life-style ideologies just mentioned, Ida was discerning and delimiting in her engagement with Korea and Korean popular culture. To Ida, this engagement largely unfolded around her fandom of Super Junior; an all-male band of up to thirteen members. Presently a university student, her engagement with this group of male K-pop performers began during her last year of high school, when a close female friend introduced her to a video in which these men performed in wigs. This is an instance of the fan service, which, as seen above, Bitten expressed her reflexive euphoria for. However, Ida's support for Super Junior did not really evolve into a more general fandom involving other aspects of Korean popular culture. Ida does not watch K-drama and expresses no particular interest in visiting Korea. She was critical about the social pressure pertinent to the beauty ideals in Korean and in K-pop, which she noted she had become aware of through her fandom.

Like Camilla, Ida's focus and productivity as a fan is predominantly channelled into the media and format of fan fiction on the international site *Asianfanfics*. Here, she has published a number of Super Junior fan fictions with genre-related tags such as 'crack fic', 'fairytale', 'angst', 'hurt and comfort', 'drama', 'romance', 'historical', 'fluff' and 'family'. Before the interview session, she recommended that I read her featured 49 chapter fan fiction, *Everyday Miracles* tagged 'fluff' and 'family'. As of August 26, 2015, *Everyday Miracles* had 255 upvotes, 870 subscribers and 51427 views **[#7]**.

During the interview session, Ida conceptualized *Everyday Miracles* as a tale of self-reflection and empowerment. In this all-male family tale, members of Super Junior are cast as fathers and sons, babysitters and friends with depictions of looks, personalities, flaws and perfections, which fans of Super Junior will pleasurably recognize. Most importantly, the story circles around existential questions as to what it means to be male and what it means to belong (to a family). Ida unfolds and explores these personal and universal themes within the typologies and narrative conventions available in the Super Junior oeuvre (MVs, TV-shows, live concerts, diverse postings on social media, other fan fictions etc.) circling around the distinctive mediated personae of the performers, within the loosely demarcated conventions of fan fiction, and through a broad orientation towards and familiarity with Western literary and screen story-worlds and conventions.

This blending of Super Junior intertextuality (fan and industry production), personal narrative and European and US literary and medial intertext gives *Everyday Miracles* a universal appeal, which is also appreciated in reader comments. As an exploration and extension of K-pop reality, this is the type of fan productivity that borders most upon conventional media and industry productiveness – not least because of the number of readers and their level of engagement in the work, as indicated by the appraisals. In a qualified sense, this makes her production comparable to non-Korean individuals like the *Eat Your Kimchi* team working professionally within and on the periphery of the K-pop industry, and, more concretely, it is an instance of how the Super Junior personae mythology is evolving both from and in between the mediated performances of the group and the trans-mediated fan productions of K-pop reality.

Jette, Karina and Line / fan productivity as reverie, career and competence building and back

The fans presented so far engaged in Korean popular culture, or some aspect of it, as an interest and hobby. Some had visited Korea briefly during summer holidays. Others had never visited and had no intention of doing so. All of them, whether critically-euphoric, mimetic, performing *ulzzang* and *aegyo*, structurally saturating their mindscapes in K-pop narratives, constructing counter-identities, being prescriptive or blurring the boundaries of fandom and industry, have immersed themselves in their respective experiences as a means in itself. In the last part of the chapter, I present three informants to whom the fan label is less obvious, but who have turned Korea into a way of life and a prospective career by obtaining places as BA students at the University of Copenhagen, majoring in Korean studies. I interviewed these three students in their second semester and again in their fourth semester.[16]

Second semester: Jette and Karina had experienced living in Korea and Japan, respectively, before embarking on Korean studies. In various ways,

16 After a guided tour at the National Museum of Denmark for the 1st year students of Korean studies, I presented my research project and asked for informants. These three students volunteered for the initial interview session.

they both had a critically euphoric approach to K-pop, K-drama and Korean popular culture comparable to that of Bitten descibed earlier in this chapter. Jette stated that when she arrived in Seoul the year after she finished high school, she realized that Korea was more than K-pop and good-looking people, and that the 'MVs create a utopia, creates a non-representative Korea.' Karina, who visited Seoul briefly during a longer stay in Japan, felt that the city seemed very grey and lifeless, not particularly sweet and warm as she had imagined it from her prior consumption of K-pop and K-drama. However, this sense of 'disillusion' did not diminish neither Jette nor Karina's interest in K-pop. They simply realized that K-pop perfectionism was not metonymically representative of Korea. It was more of a media universe in its own terms.

Bitten's observations of the way in which some Danish fangirls adored the versatility and liberalism of Korean masculinities may fit into the critique of orientalist fantasies and stereotyping outlined in *Migrants, fans and cultural critique*. Likewise, the fans I interviewed gave plenty of examples of how they had experienced prejudices, not least from young Danish males commenting on what they considered the emasculated masculinity of K-pop performers, which may be categorized as Hübinette's 'gook humour.' For our purposes, and in all its rationality, the distinction made by these students between Hallyu and its pop perfectionism and the 'real Korea' is central as it makes it unfeasible to categorize and critique this particular form of consumption as embodying any kind of perceived representativeness in terms of Danish orientalist fantasies and appropriations of Korea. To the students, these two worlds are discernible, overlapping and co-existent in the same entangled manner as Hollywood and the US is to 'mainstream' Danish consumers.

As first year students, a strong sense of community and shared experience permeated their communication, and key points of reference in this community were K-pop, K-drama, fashion and humour related to awkward English in K-pop and other factors. Karina emphasized the radical innovation of the K-pop universe and used eating-related metaphors to elaborate on this: 'a large upgraded Kinder chocolate egg', 'a sugar explosion', 'served with a spoon', which nicely highlights the seductiveness and the mediated carnal pleasure, as well as the child-like positionality and excessiveness experienced by female consumers of versatile Korean masculinities **[#8]**. Fan productivity on these terms was identifiable as a pleasurable and excessive experience in itself, but also a mutually motivating feature of studies and hobby, in effect making it into a way of life, as Jette explained. Line, who did not share this interest, related how the ubiquity of media referencing was something the non-fan students had to find a way of relating to in order to fit into the student community **[#9]**.

On a small scale, this mediated referencing further attests to a shift in Korean-Danish relations in which Korea as dreamscape and cultural geography is at the moment contributing to change West–to–East cultural flows, and doing it in a way in which we cannot possibly reduce the agency of K-pop fans to post-colonial fantasies and appropriations. Concretely, it has the contours of a Korean dream in the form of ambitions about entering the Hallyu industry professionally.

Fourth semester: The first interview session found the students as Hallyu consumers at a de-enchanted yet euphoric stage. The following year, I re-interviewed Jette after her return from Seoul, and Karina and Line during their second semester in Seoul. Interestingly, their intense communal experience of K-pop reality produced through the consumption of K-pop and K-drama in Denmark subsided once they were in Seoul. Notably, in the case of all three, having to cope with everyday life in Seoul with all its linguistic, cultural and social challenges, forced K-pop and K-drama away from its central position to the extent of almost evaporating from everyday life. Line remarked that K-pop was even more annoying to her now, and Jette said that she spent so much energy on keeping up with life in Korea that there was nothing left for K-drama and K-pop. Instead, she had relaxed with English language dramas and music **[#10]**. Friendships with Korean students and adults were also not based on communal consumption of K-pop and K-drama. Line added that her Korean friends disliked K-pop.

Another notable shift is the perception and practice of Korean sociality. Jette, for instance, reflected upon how, during her stay, she gradually came to accept and partially practice a set of beauty ideal practices – not least by frequently visiting beauty salons; she also considered getting a nose-job to obtain a smaller, more 'Korean' nose. Upon returning to Copenhagen, she re-discovered K-pop and K-drama and swiftly abandoned any ideas about plastic surgery.

These positional shifts between what I have broadly termed K-pop reality and Korean sociality are highly complex. For our purposes, suffice it to say that these movements between the Danish student community setting and life as an exchange student in Seoul indicate how an Asian modernity in all its complexity has become a wider repertoire for Danish productive fans in reflecting on their own lives and society in light of East Asian modernities (Iwabuchi 2013: 51). These shifts, in other words, are important in accessing the trans-Asian mediated referencing of Danish productive fans. Firstly, they show that the formation of intimacy and engagement is not simply steadily progressing towards a fixed goal, but is a fluctuating state of mind which allows for shifting perceptions in the pendular movement between Copenhagen and Seoul. Secondly, these shifts show us that the dissimilarity between K-pop reality and Korean sociality is something that fans are reflecting on and act upon to differing degrees.

Korean Dreams and K-Pop Realities

The term 'K-pop reality' denotes how the Danish fans in this study engage with the Hallyu dreamscape. This kind of engagement is characteristic of both the mimetic, critically euphoric, the prescriptive and counter-identity conscious fans. The dreamscape is enabled by a highly innovative and market-sensitive Korean cultural industry, which collaborates with and integrates Japanese and Western media systems, soundscapes and sensibilities into its products. It is a dreamscape which makes available attractive masculinities, engaging narratives and flawless flaws. A dreamscape in which the predominantly early 20s female Danish fans of this study produce fan fiction, cover dance, websites, social narratives, as well as ever-expanding materialities, discourses and sensibilities.

From this perspective, the fan typology and its interconnectedness with a reversal of transnational flows is worthy of note. It demonstrates the emergence of Danish youths, who, to varying degrees of intensity and by dissimilar means, identify with and belong to the loose cultural geography of Korea and East Asia. They aspire to integrate into the Korean social fabric through career choice, and they produce K-pop realities by performing Korean dance, conforming to Korean aesthetics or beauty ideals, thinking through Korean story-worlds and finding viable alternatives to Danish youth sociality. I have mainly explored this productivity as formative of K-pop reality. The 'Korean dream' description is, on the other hand, a pun on the American Dream, which has a strong, rhetorical resonance in post-Korean War South Korean society, and multiple associations to compressed modernity, upward social mobility and social ambition. Again, the presence of a counter-flow, which goes from East to the West, makes it worthwhile reconsidering the scholarship that sees cultural appropriation, everyday racism, fetishism, exoticism and imperialism in Western cultural appropriations and representations of Korea among Asian non-(im)migrants in the West. As argued throughout this book, the fans and their voices and narratives as explored here are moved by and form (K-pop) realities that do not quite fit into this explanatory frame.

Revisiting Iwabuchi's notion of the inter-Asian mediated referencing, we have seen how the mediated encounter with Asian modernities through the consumption of TV dramas, film and popular music offers Danish fans a wider repertoire for reflecting on their own lives and societies in light of East Asian modernities. Iwabuchi suggested that '...[t]he inclusion of Asian migrants living in Western countries in trans-Asian cultural connection would be imperative to go beyond a closed conception of "Asia" as a region' (2015: 7). In short, I have argued here that, through Danish productive fans, their K-pop reality and trans-Asian mediated referencing, we may find ways to go further beyond this closed conception of "Asia" as a region.

Bibliography

Chen, Kuan-Hsing. 2010. *Asia as method: toward deimperialization*. Durham: Duke University Press.

Cho, Younghan. 2011. "Desperately seeking East Asia amidst the popularity of South Korean pop culture in Asia". *Cultural Studies* 25 (3): 383–404.

Chua, Beng Huat. 2012. *Structure, audience and soft power in East Asian pop culture*. Hong Kong: Hong Kong University Press.

Chua, Beng Huat. 2008. "Structure of Identification and Distancing in Watching East Asian Television Drama" in B.H. Chua & K. Iwabuchi (eds.) *East Asian pop culture: analysing the Korean wave*. Hong Kong: Hong Kong University Press, pp.73–89.

Chua, Beng Huat & Koichi Iwabuchi (eds.) 2008. *East Asian pop culture: analysing the Korean wave*. Hong Kong: Hong Kong University Press

Condry, Ian. 2006. *Hip-hop Japan: rap and the paths of cultural globalization*. Durham: Duke University Press.

Hellekson, Karen & Kristina Busse. 2014. *The Fan Fiction Studies Reader*. Iowa City: University of Iowa Press.

Hübinette, Tobias. 2012. "The Reception and Consumption of Hallyu in Sweden: Preliminary Findings and Reflections". *Korea Observer* 43 (3): 503–525.

Iwabuchi, Koichi. 2015. "Modernity, Dialogue, and Re-nationalization: Critical Issues in the Study of Trans-Asian Media Culture Connections". *Asian Journal of Journalism and Media Studies* (2015): 1–16.

Iwabuchi, Koichi. 2014. "De-westernisation, inter-Asian referencing and beyond". *European Journal of Cultural Studies* 17 (1): 44–57.

Iwabuchi, Koichi. 2013. "Korean Wave and inter-Asian referencing" in: Kim, Youna (ed.). *The Korean wave: Korean media go global*. London and New York: Routledge, pp.43–57.

Iwabuchi, Koichi. 2010. "Undoing International Fandom in the Age of Brand Nationalism". *Mechademia* 5: 86–96.

Iwabuchi, Koichi. 2010a. "De-Westernization and the governance of global cultural connectivity: a dialogic approach to East Asian media cultures". *Postcolonial Studies.* 13 (4): 403–419.

Iwabuchi, Koichi. 2002. *Recentering globalization: popular culture and Japanese transnationalism.* Durham: Duke University Press.

Jenkins, Henry. 2006. *Fans, bloggers, and gamers: exploring participatory culture.* New York: New York University Press.

Jenkins, Henry. 1992. *Textual poachers: television fans & participatory culture.* New York: Routledge.

Jenkins, Henry, Sam Ford & Joshua Green. 2013. *Spreadable media: creating value and meaning in a networked culture.* New York: New York University Press.

Jung, Eun-Young. 2013. "K-pop female idols in the West: racial imaginations and erotic fantasies" in: Kim, Youna (ed.). *The Korean wave: Korean media go global.* London and New York: Routledge, pp.106–119.

Jung, Sun. 2011. *Korean masculinities and transcultural consumption: Yonsama, Rain, Oldboy, K-Pop Idols.* Hong Kong: Hong Kong University Press.

Kim, Youna. 2013. *The Korean wave: Korean media go global.* London and New York: Routledge.

Kim, Youna. 2013a. "Korean media in a digital cosmopolitan world" in: Kim, Youna (ed.). *The Korean wave: Korean media go global.* London and New York: Routledge. pp.1–27.

Kim, Youna. 2013b. "Korean Wave pop culture in the global Internet age" in: Kim, Youna (ed.). *The Korean wave: Korean media go global.* London and New York: Routledge. pp.75–92.

Park, Jung-Sun. 2013. "Negotiating identity and power in transnational cultural consumption: Korean American youths and the Korean Wave in: Kim, Youna (ed.). *The Korean wave: Korean media go global.* London and New York: Routledge. pp.120–134.

Petersen, Martin. (Forthcoming). *Purikura.* Odense: University Press of Southern Denmark.

Petersen, Martin. (Forthcoming). *Museum Manhwa.* Odense: University Press of Southern Denmark.

Petersen, Martin. 2022. *Cosplay.* Odense: University Press of Southern Denmark.

Petersen, Martin. 2011. "Collecting Korean shamanism for the National Museum of Denmark: ethnographic objects as collecting devices". *Nordisk Museologi 2011* (2): 48–66.

Petersen, Martin. 2008. *Collecting Korean Shamanism: biographies & collecting devices: four collections of Ethnographic objects in the National Museum of Denmark.* Copenhagen: Det Humanistiske Fakultet, Københavns Universitet.

Sung, Sang-Yeon. 2013. "Digitization and online cultures of the Korean Wave: "East Asian" virtual community in Europe" in: Kim, Youna (ed.). *The Korean wave: Korean media go global.* Londo and New York: Routledge, pp.135–147.

Yu, Ishikawa. 2010. "Yaoi as Fanwork: Cultural Appropriation in Modern Japanese Culture". *Journal of Urban Culture Research* 1: 170–177.

Korean Dreams and K-pop Realities: A supplement

[#1] A topography of Danish fans ... an afternoon stroll through the King's Garden / Bitten

Martin: If I walked through the King's Garden, would I be able to distinguish the different fan groups?

Bitten: Well, I am there [in the King's Garden] with those who are into Korean pop music. We started out being around twenty. But we grew in numbers. We are twenty to thirty people. Even if there are 700-800 hundred in the [Facebook] group [Danish K-pop Lovers] now, that's the number of people who join [the meet-up].

For one reason or another ... people who are fans of Korean pop music they are really against, well ... for example Beliebers [Justin Bieber fans] and Directioners [One Direction fans]. It's just a no-go. They just say it out loud when they walk by. And it's kind of strange because they are all alike somehow. I think that maybe they [the Beliebers and Directioners] group us with cosplayers. Now, I'm not a fan of Justin Bieber or anything but they are quite cool. His fans are quite cool. They are extremely well organized. Last time I saw them in the King's Garden, they had this whole line-up. Someone stood in the front and then they had rows of fans who stood there and learned a choreography. They all learned his choreography in rows. It was really awesome.

Directioners usually march down through the King's Garden. They have a D written on their cheeks and they have big banners. And there are lots and lots of their fans. But typically younger girls. Beliebers and Directioners typically are the younger crowd. The K-pop group is a bit more anonymous because it is such a small group. Typically, it is people,

who are dressed in the same fashion as in Korea. Martina from *Eat Your Kimchi* [a popular YouTube channel] is a huge inspiration. In the way she styles her hair... She has these hair tutorials, which you can learn from and she's dying her hair pink. So, they do not stand out as much as the cosplay group which is also there. The cosplay group is a bit more … well … You're always able to recognize them. They're always in cosplay.

They blend a bit into the goth group which is also in the King's Garden. It's funny. They [the cosplayers] come over to us all of the time. They are enormously kind people; extrovert people. They are dropping by when we are having a meet-up, and we sit there eating cake. "Oh, heey! What's up." Maybe they know someone in our group, who is then kinda trying: "Oh no, the cosplayers are coming." Then "Ignore!" and these cosplayers come by and "Heeeey!" There are many in the K-pop group who recognize their former self in them. I also feel that way. They feel that they are not like that any longer. They've left behind this tremendously extroverted way of being. It's like. "I'm too cool for that." And we are just sitting under a tree eating cake. [Laughing out loud]. That's more or less what we are doing.

No, well, we're also dancing. Typically there is this list. There is a list that you enter your music on. Otherwise it's impossible to know what to play as people are fans of all different kinds of things. Then we turn on the music and just let it play. And there are many who can dance to the songs and then either they are dancing together or just alone. Some people know all the dances or the chorus of the songs. It is really … It is very nice and cozy … We're talking about the shows we're watching. And sometimes we make competitions with posters someone brought. And we also copy some of the games they do in Korean TV shows … And also there are people, who are doing covers, who have YouTube channels where they are singing the Korean songs in Danish […]

LUCIFER

[Then talking about dance covers] My friend, Dora, I've made dance covers with her. She practiced. And she knows these dances. We went shooting a video at the graffiti wall behind the Dong Energy building. An incredibly nice place. Then I shot her dance, and she put it on her YouTube channel and I did the same, and we got quite a positive response. It's just kind of our project [...]

Where did we come from ... The King's Garden and K-pop meet-ups. Those who came to K-pop from cosplay... The funny thing is that they want to stand out but not negatively. They [the K-pop fans] are much more self-conscious. Whereas the cosplayers typically just want to stand out. Do something which makes them visible. 'Look what I'm doing in my free time.' Those who are into K-pop are typically keen on sharing their interest for Korea and K-pop. They wish there would be more K-pop fans. And in a way it's funny that they want the number of K-pop fans to grow and yet they also want to be special. So, if there are many K-pop fans, it's not so cool. When PSY came out with Gangnam Style, it was really controversial. Because he came out with a song which was globally popular but the fans, they were like ... There was a big discussion. People got really upset.

[#2] Roads into Korea and Hallyu ... it starts with Japan / Bitten

Martin: How did you discover Korea?

Bitten: It was through Japan. I was also interested in anime and manga. And then it just became Asian culture in general. I listened to Japanese music all through 7th to 9th grade [of compulsory School] and then through that I also somehow came across Korean pop music. And I was like: "Nooooo. Korean pop." I also started learning Japanese language, I studied it for one year and there were also some girls in my class who were interested in Korean pop music.

[#3] Feelings of imtimacy and the humanness of K-pop stars … on watching the boy band ShiNee in the reality show 'Hello Baby' / Dora

Dora: So, they are put into all kinds of situations. And they have to take care of this child. And then it's more like – I think it's fun to watch. You see all the members … who is who and how they act in different situations.

[Talking about a ShiNee music video] It shows the band where they are like "We're so perfect. We can sing. We can dance. We can do anything. Be good-looking." And then [in 'Hello Baby'] they come into these situations where you can see that sometimes … What I like about K-pop is that with many of the Western artists you only see their stardom. You only see when they are good looking. But here [in 'Hello Baby'], there are cases where they are woken up in the morning without make-up on. And you can see that they are thinking "Oh no. This is not good." You get all the way around them; what are they like when they are tired. Who's making dinner. You can also see how they interact together. Who gets along better with who and who they prefer to be with.

[#4] Uneasy encounters with mainstream youth culture and feeling stereotyped / Dora

Dora: You're often put in a box when you say: "I like K-pop." I remember that I told my high school class mates. I began listening to K-pop in the last year of compulsory school. I did not really talk about it. And then I entered high school and did not have a lot of self-confidence. I told myself to be self-confident and not to care about what other people said as I already had friends who liked me for who I am. So I knew that I was ok. And then when I told them … . it was not like I just came out and said: "Hey. K-pop. Yes. Man. Come on!" It was more like [I was telling it to] one person at a time. And then all my class mates found out. It happened when I posted my first [K-pop cover] dance [video] on Facebook and I didn't see that it was posted in an open group. And then next day they had all seen it ... Often you are put in a box: "Oh! So you like to cosplay." They think that the costumes are weird. "How come you like Chinese?" And you are like: "It is not Chinese. [Sighs subdued] It is Korean." I've also been asked: "Oh. So you just want to have an Asian boyfriend?" Nooo! It has got nothing to do with that. I've got to admit that if I see an Asian walking down the street I might give the person a second look ... But it's got nothing to do with that. And then there is the standard comment: "But you don't know what they're singing."

[#5] Korean fashion and *ulzzang* - 'The Korean fashion style – it is a lot about having a flawless face' / Gene

Gene: I am a person who is madly into Asian fashion style. I am a member of a [Facebook] group called 'Asian Fashion Style in Denmark'. We are approximately 600 members. It is Asian fashion. It's not only Korean but also Japanese. The majority follows the Japanese fashion style. Korean culture is not as popular as the Japanese.

I order a lot of clothes online. Not from Korean [pages] but from E-Bay and some Asian pages. I simply buy the clothes which are nice and which I can use for Korean fashion or just generally Asian.

I strive to follow this style, which is called *ulzzang* in Korea. It actually means 'best face'. The face must look very v-line, with a slim nose and then be as cute as possible. In this new culture, that is the modern culture, it has become defined as a style and not just the face.

I've showed some photos of [Korean] girls to my classmates ... and they just think that they are Barbie dolls and that it looks unnatural. Their faces ... it seems like they are going for a doll [look] in that way, right.

I'm going for the natural look. If it wasn't because I'm chubby, I think

I would have had a slightly v-lined face. I think, maybe. I'm one of those stereotypes who wants to look like them as much as possible. I'm also wearing contact lenses and such things. And then I'm also wearing make-up ... foundation or whitening cream to look more white.

I get a lot of comments on my fashion style. The main point of my fashion style is that I like to dress in nice clothes and to make it look more Asian than just ordinary, nice fashion style. For example, I like these Asian school uniforms; both Japanese and Korean, and then I try to make it look Asian. Some people say that the main point about Asian fashion style is the clothes. For me it's actually about the face, the make-up and the hair style. Because that's actually what makes you look Asian. If I saw a K-pop star who wore some clothes then I'd say K-pop style, but if I saw a Dane or European who was wearing it then I'd say it was normal.

[#6] K-pop as a transnational connection / Helen

Helen: When you like K-pop it opens a lot of doors and you enter a completely different universe. And just the thing about meeting people – they don't even have to like K-pop. It's people from Malaysia, Taiwan, all other kinds of places. This thing about meeting them in real life and be with them – now, I've met really a lot of my friends [in this way] and it's simply fantastic to have so much in common, while it does not have to be K-pop. It can also be something else. We have so many other things in common. For example, what I fear personally or dislike, what I like, what my strengths are. I really have a lot in common with these people. And, yes, I think that's really cool. And then there's another thing, which really turns me off a lot ... for example, with Denmark and that is things like how many you can fuck, how many you can have sex with. How often are you going out ... How much can you drink ... How much can you smoke and so on and so on. Whereas in Korea, it's almost shameful to

have sex before marriage. And it's not so much that I'm very traditional, but somehow I find it totally un-charming and groce to do something like that. Yes. It's completely off the rails.

We're also not hanging out on a Thursday night and getting completely wasted or high. You just don't do that in K-pop. We drink bubble tea.

[#7] *Everyday Miracles* Prelude:

- Can a broken family be mended again?
- Can the broken trust of innocent children be restored again?
- Can a stranger turn the everyday life of a family upside down?
- Can he somehow be the missing puzzle piece that keeps the family together?

Join this family on a journey filled with the smallest miracles of life, the ones we do not always notice, the ones that put a smile on the face of those who do. The simple *everyday miracles*

[#8] Consuming K-pop / Karina

Karina [on her first encounter with Korea]: That's the thing with Korea. Compared to China and Japan, Korea's got the full package. You get all the sweet stuff also found in Japan. And then you get history and culture also found in China. You can listen to pop music. You can listen to hip hop. You can listen to rock. You can listen to all genres. You get visuals; their looks. There is fashion, there is food. There is … well, there is everything. Where … if it's Japan, then it's mostly J-pop that people listen to. J-pop just doesn't catch me. It's a bit too odd. And sweet in a kind of strange way. And then there's a bit of film and TV-drama, but otherwise not so much. With China there's a bit of film and maybe a little bit with the music. But what I've heard is not so varied. Whereas in Korea you get ALL the best from all the different fields. And I think that's probably the reason why many end up with Korea. It's one large upgraded Kinder-egg. There's the sweet on the outside and the surprise on the inside. So it's a constant surprise. Even if you listen to the same group, then each time they come out with something new. You have no idea what to expect. It's so innovative all the time. Then they change hair colour, style, outfit. And the sound is also constantly changing. So, that's exciting. Even if it's not the coolest song they have made, then as they've made a new, interesting music video, it's still cool to watch because it's new.

What we [talking about her Korean studies class mates] are focusing on at the moment is the picture postcard. It's the Kinder-egg that we're eating raw. Eating it all up […] When will we be full … that's a pretty good question. J-rock died out at a point. It was really big at some point and then it just kind of died out. And the same thing with K-pop; will it die out at some point? But then we talked about how, as soon as K-pop starts to fade, then the music companies come up with something new. Then they come up with something we haven't seen before and then it goes up again. And they just do that every time it starts fading, then they throw something new out at us. Really, we're like hungry lions who are being fed meat and we throw ourselves upon it. But it's a picture postcard. It's sugar. There are also really many negative things about Korea.

[#9] On the importance of Korean popular culture – the TV-dramas, the music to the Korean studies student community / Line and Jette

Line: It is a very, very central part. Many students have chosen Korean Studies because they like the popular culture. That's how they discovered it. And if we have a Christmas party, then we're listening to K-pop. It is a big common denominator. And well, some of us did not know about it beforehand and yet we embraced it. And we're also singing along. And I do also find it very funny when they're singing in broken English in those K-pop songs. Then we really feel that this is the coolest thing we've ever done. It's addictive.

Jette: Before I entered Korean Studies I did not watch K-dramas. I had an expectation that it was sugar sweet. That is was this bubblegum universe, and I was thinking: "I'm not quite sure about it. I don't want to focus on that." It was not until I came back to Denmark and entered Korean Studies and the other girls were talking a lot about K-drama that I thought ... well ... since everyone is talking about it, maybe I should give it a try anyway. So I do think that we are addicting each other a lot.

Line: We're posting a lot of stuff to each other on Facebook. "See this silly video" and such strange things. It's all the fault of the internet.

Jette: [laughs]

[#10] After an exchange semester in Seoul / Jette

Jette: When I returned to South Korea ... we listened to K-pop at first. Initially, we lived in a hostel and listened to K-pop and cultivated our bubble. But when we moved into a university dorm and the semester started, we established an everyday life and a daily rhythm. Then I think ... since there was so much Korean around me all the time, I started listening more to English language music. And rather than watching K-dramas as I do here in Denmark I also started watching more English language dramas. Because ... I had to relax my brain once in a while. It really takes a lot to concentrate on Korean all the time. Also because when I had just arrived in Korea I spent a lot of energy on picking up conversations around me – trying to make sense of them. I spent a lot of energy on that and I was tired to the bone in the beginning until I thought to myself ... I was lying in bed trying to follow the Korean dramas and thinking "I just can't", "I just can't." And then I began watching some series in English and listened more to English language music instead and I did not feel as tired during the day. So, I was able to better focus on my studies, and I could better focus on my friendships and stuff like that. And I thought: "That's the way it is. So. That's the way to do it."

TAO

Danish Hallyu fandom in perspective

This section features three portraits of persons, who engage in K-pop in various ways. The first portrait is of six Hungarian fans, whom I interviewed on June 17, 2015 in Budapest. The second portrait is of Danish musician, songwriter and producer Thomas Troelsen, whose activities as a songwriter include working with K-pop bands such as SHINee and Super Junior under the major Korean music company, SM Entertainment. I spoke to him on February 20, 2015. The third portrait is of Creative Chief and Head of A&R, Chris Sung-su Lee, SM Entertainment, whom I met on March 24, 2005. Apart from SHINee and Super Junior, EXO and Girls' Generation are also associated with SM Entertainment. The section concludes with a lengthy excerpt from my conversation with Chris Sung-su Lee.

These portraits of the Hungarian fans and the two professionals involved in the Korean music industry indicate what I will term 'triple abandonment'; that is, national, creative and commercial abandonment.

Portrait one: National abandonment / Hungarian Fans

In Budapest on June 17, 2015, I met six members of the Hungarian fan groups 2HEXO, Yehet Dance and Hungarian Hallyu Headquarters (HHHQ). 2HEXO is a fan group of the male K-pop group EXO, Yehet Dance is a Hungarian K-pop cover dance group and, lastly, HHHQ organizes Korean popular cultural events.[17]

Entering the conversation with a familiarity with Danish Hallyu fans, my encounter with the Hungarian fans very much felt like a move through familiar terrain. The way that the six friends talked about their fandom, their idols, shared their experiences, as well as their sense of humor, made me somewhat oblivious to the shift in national setting from Copenhagen to Bu-

17 Two informants were members of 2HEXO, five were members of Yehet Dance and one was a member of HHHQ.

dapest. I also recognized the features of mimetic and euphoric-reflexive fans identified in Danish Hallyu fandom. Based on just one interview session, it is not the aim here to draw comparisons with the typology of Danish fans. In one respect, however, there was a marked difference to the Danish fans.

Hungarian Hallyu fandom is more organized, and the fan base is larger. A case in point, there are professional and semi-professional organizations, which engage the Hallyu fandom. The Korean Cultural Center in Budapest makes Korea accessible to the Hungarian public.[18] Among its many-faceted activities are also K-pop activities. This includes making dance studio facilities available, making dance classes available and hosting K-pop events and the like. The six Hungarian fans had joined various activities by the Korean Cultural Center. Further, there is a Budapest based company, Idolater, which collaborates with the Cultural Center in attempting to establish contact between the centre and various Hungarian as well as other European fan groups.[19] The Yehet Dance members also expressed a sense of competitiveness and semi-professionalization; they participate in national cover-dance festivals and K-pop festivals and in this context debate the criteria for judging cover-dance performances. In sum, the six fans appeared to be more directly targeted by and logistically linked up with agencies and institutions representing a Korean national soft power agenda and neo-liberal entrepreneurship than I experienced was the case with Danish fans.

---

18 The Korean Cultural Centers are run by the *Korean Culture and Information Service*, a subdivision of South Korea's *Ministry of Culture, Sports and Tourism*. As part of efforts to introduce and spread interest in diverse aspects of Korean culture, the centres have organized many programs under the categories of arts, music, literature, film and cuisine.

19 "We unite the European K-pop fan groups by organizing official K-pop events like concerts, fan projects, K-pop camps, fan meetings, K-pop workshops and we keep strong communication between them and the K-pop world. [...] Even though there are lots fans in Europe, by not communicating with each other and not forming a unit, they stay almost invisible for the Korean market. Recognizing the problem mentioned above, we decided to establish a team who is determined to connect the Hungarian and European fans with the Korean communities". (https://idolaterevents.com/about/about-the-team/)

Portrait Two: Creative abandonment / Thomas Troelsen

I have previously mentioned how non-Korean persons like the Canadian bloggers from *Eat Your Kimchi* are situated in between Hallyu, Korea and the K-pop industry on one hand and Danish fans on the other; an inter-mediating role from which Korea and Korean popular culture become translated, understandable and more easily consumable for many fans. There are, however, also non-Asian individuals working within the K-pop industry. The Danish songwriter Thomas Troelsen is one among the Scandinavian and other European and American songwriters who contribute to the soundscape of K-pop. In this capacity, Thomas Troelsen is interesting for two reasons here.

Firstly, he is an embodiment of the transnationalism, which is present in K-pop in a range of ways. This opens up for ways to reconsider notions of national culture and trans-Asian mediated referencing in its geographically bounded meaning not only in the fan-base but also within the industry.

Secondly, Troelsen is interesting in terms of his working method, which is shaped by the creative freedom given him by SM Entertainment. During our conversation, he said that it was a conscious choice on his part to not produce music which departs from within the existing K-pop soundscape nor for that matter to gain familiarity with Korea or Korean culture through research or visits. On the contrary, Troelsen's creative work for SM Entertainment was a kind of tabula rasa; in his own words, in the creation process he imagined various scenarios, among these scenarios that he was making striptease music for the 22nd century. Taken at face value, this singular statement makes Troelsen's contribution to the 'Korean' soundscape, the sound of Korea, a truly cosmopolitan matter; an artistic vision in which neither Korean nor, for that matter, Danish fans were pre-conceived as consumers.

Portrait Three: Commercial abandonment / SM Entertainment

Seen from those perspectives, while the K-pop universe is certainly permeated by national and capital interests, the Danish K-pop fans were relatively 'left alone' by Korean national agencies and, at least in Troelsen's case, not part of the creative vision. A conversation with Creative Chief and Head of A&R, Chris Sung-su Lee from SM Entertainment, further underlined this peripheral position of Danish fans. Lee emphasized that, currently, his company did not have the European (much less the Danish K-pop) fans in mind when making their productions.

SM Entertainment, while having an internationalist outlook and a global focus in terms of making products, which everyone can consume and enjoy, were at the time of the interview focusing on the Asian market, in particular on China. Yet (or perhaps, by contrast), Europe had a great symbolical significance. As a point in case, Lee emphasized the SM Town concerts in Paris 2011 as milestones in the European recognition and discovery of K-pop and Hallyu. Also, he highlighted as something very significant the fact that many European artists were working in the production of K-pop. However, the incorporation of European and other non-Korean artists into the 'Korean' product was done predominantly with an Asian, and not least Chinese, market in mind. That this feature also seemingly became part of the attractiveness of the product to European consumer, needless to say, was a welcome side-effect.

In sum, these three portraits indicate the relative abandonment of Danish fans by national, creative and commercial interests. I am not suggesting that this triple abandonment in itself is formative of these fans and their productiveness, which we will explore in Part Two. However, from this position in a peripheral market and a 'far-away' country, the Danish fans arguably have a stimulus to build their individual experience with and communal life around K-pop and Hallyu around the sense of sharing their fandom and the on-going discovery of this universe with a selected few.

Chris Lee , SM Entertainment on European K-pop fans

Martin: How do you see the European market and how do you see the European fan?

Chris Lee: Basically, it's not that we don't have any interest in the European countries, but as you know, we are also a corporation; profit-seeking. Therefore, we have to also consider the costs we have to invest to gain some profit from certain markets. When we look at the European market, the issue is that, compared to other markets, the population number that reside in the European continent, the [amount] of music they consume is not as great. Hence when we consider all the pros and the cons in the investment we have to make to break through the European market, for instance selling physical copies of our albums and so on, we figured that it would be more economical for us to concentrate on certain other markets like China and therefore create a bigger profit.

The European market has two main significances to us. Number one, in the symbolic way that, because people consider that a culturally significant place, then when we go to Europe we get more attention and it signifies the success that we've been having internationally. For instance, when we had the SM Town Concert in Paris in 2011. That's when we started to really receive international attention on what is K-pop and what SM did to foster Hallyu, so in that way Europe has that symbolical significance to us.

Secondly, and more importantly, we feel that ... what we're trying to find in Europe is original sound – the originality of the music that we bring into Korea and then when we bring in this music to Korea we localize it and make it suitable for the Asian market. But the fact that the European fans are responding to our music that means ... also for instance Thomas Troelsen ... it means that what we have localized, what we thought we have localized for Asian market is also working vice versa. We can assess how much international response we can get from our K-pop through the way that the European consumers react to our music and our products. So in those two ways, Europe is significant, symbolically, to us [...]

SM Entertainment is the company which has the technology, which we call CT – Cultural Technology. We call it CT but it's producing skill. So we are the company that has this producing skill. We know how we can produce all the music, with the choreography and the music video et cetera et cetera. But we are not writers. SM Entertainment is the producer, but we are not writers. We employ the writers who have 'the future eyes' which actually nobody thinks about because that's what people are really interested in – or they can [feel that] "Oh, it's cool!" So, whenever we talk with the writer, we never give them any specifics and that's how we have been doing for the last, over twenty years.

One of the keys to our success was the great sounds that we received from international writers, for example in Denmark, Sweden and [other] Scandinavian countries, and also with our good artists and with our Cultural Technology in a mixture that has enabled us to prosper in the market. But also our head producer Mr. Sung Man Lee – this company is named after him – has been in the centre of the whole producing process from the beginning to the end and he's even still active until now. So he's also the inspiration and key to the success that we have been enjoying in the market.

Part Two: Collection Catalogue: Fan Productions and Interviews

Introduction

This part presents the National Museum of Denmark Hallyu fandom collection. The collection consists of a small selection of creative Danish fan productions. These examples of fan productivity are material, textual and medial. They are organized into four sections: Fan accessories, fan fiction, cover dance and fan art.

'Fan accessories' presents an example of a fan production which has become part of everyday life in the fan community – a self-made deck of cards. 'Fan fiction' showcases excerpts from three stories. 'Cover dance' features a fan-made cover dance video. Lastly, 'Fan art' exemplifies how K-pop stars are rendered by Danish fans exemplified through two water-colours.

This 'fan productivity' collection and its interrelation with K-pop reality and trans-Asian mediated referencing is contexualized in each section through extensive excerpts from conversations I have had with fans on their material, textual and medial creations.

Fan accessories

On June 1, 2014, I interviewed the two long-time friends, Bitten and Dora. At one point in our conversation, they talked about male K-pop band members and how these members relate to one another in the band. Fans create imaginative couples, or 'ships' as they call them, where two members have or perform a fond and warm connection. This led us on to talk about fan fiction where these ships are explored. Dora laughingly denies any familiarity with fan fiction and clarifies how, instead, she has become familiar with them through a deck of cards made by Bitten.

Interview with Bitten and Dora

Dora: I only know the couples because everybody's shipping them. The only reason I know the couples is because she [indicating Bitten] has this deck of cards at home where the couple names are written and then there are photos of them. Well!!!!

Martin: You made them yourself?

Bitten: There are all these ships ... 'ships' means that you have two persons and then you match them up in a couple ... it's a naval fleet. So, it is a ship which you are shipping from ....

Martin: Did you make your own playing cards?

Bitten: [Yes]. It is something where you can say ... if it's a comic it would have been called canon. It is the official couples. Eunhyuk and Donghae [two members of Super Junior]. There is one ship called Eunhae [Eunhyuk/ Donghae]. Since they have been in business for such a long time they know that the fans are shipping them; putting them together as a couple. They also have a duo called "Eunhae". They have made music together.

Dora: At concerts you can also see them doing all sorts of things.

Martin: They get that the fans are shipping them and then they actually do it in variety shows and the like?

Bitten: Yes, yes. They are responding to it. ... It's interactive.

Dora: Actually, at the concert [Dora went to a Super Junior concert in Berlin] Well, I didn't see it because it was at exactly that moment that Siwon threw off his shirt. Wuiii. He was also at bit closer. Well, apparently Donghae went over to Eunhyuk with a water bottle ... Eunhyuk then looked at him with eyes saying "You're dead if you do it". And then he [Donghae] poured water over him and then he ran away from Eunhyuk.

Bitten: I imagine that the fans were …

Dora: Yes. It was like: 'iyaaaaaaaaa'.

Martin: That's also a kind of fan service.

Dora and Bitten: Yes! Yes!

Bitten: And then they have … there is always kind of a different dynamic in a group … these roles. For example, in EXO there is a mom and a dad …

Martin: [Returning to the topic of the playing cards] Can you buy them in stores or is it [only] some that you made yourself?

Bitten: What I did was to take a deck of cards. Then I bought polish and printed a lot of pictures in the same format; with the same measures as playing cards, which I glued them on and then polished. I have … in principle there are 52 cards in a deck and then 26 pairs. One row is with pictures. That is pictures of their ship.

Dora: And it's not just pictures. It's pictures where their ship is really there.

Martin: But you chose these pictures yourself?

Bitten: It is really easy. You just search on their … couple names. Donghae / Eunhyuk: Eunhae … You can also just do a search on Super Junior couples. … They have those couple names because these are the couples, which are shipped the most. There are also some [K-pop stars] where you can … well … funnily enough, Shindong [ed. member of Super Junior] is not in a couple with anyone. He is kind of a bit on his own. But it varies a lot, who is talking and hanging out together, then there is an official [couple] … there are some where people are saying "This is a must couple in Super Junior". Then I've made pictures of them, and on [another card] I've written their couple names, and then written who is in the couple and which group they are from. And it is a deck of cards where you can play memory game, Old Maid and Go Fish with them, for example.

JONGTAE
JONGHYUN/TAEMIN
(SHINEE)
TAEKAI
TAEMIN/KAI
(SHINEE/EXO)
EUNSIHAE
EUNHYUK/SIWON/DONGHA
(SUPER JUNIOR)
YOOSU
YOOCHUN/JUNSU
(TVXQ)
SICHUL
SIWON/HEECHUL
(SUPER JUNIOR)
83-LINE
LEETEUK/HEECHUL
(SUPER JUNIOR)
(SUPER JUNIOR)
NOOTHERFAA

Dora: All you need to do is to find out who is the Old Maid ... it's a bit like who wouldn't you like to have in your hand. You want to have all on them in your hand [laughs].

Bitten: It's really fun to play with other fangirls because they all have their own favourite ship. It is like 'noooooo'.

Dora: I want those!!! [screaming the names of the band members]

Bitten: I've made it with four groups from SM Town: SHINee, Donghwa, txq, Super Junior ...

Martin: Are you replacing the cards with new ones ...

Bitten: I should but I'm not.

Dora: As long as it's not with girls [from female K-pop bands] because with them I have no clue who is who.

Martin: There are no girls in this deck?

Bitten: Nooo. But I know that the boys [male K-pop fans] also ship the girls. And there are all kinds of rumors that Tifanny and Taeyon [from Girls' Generation] are also in a relationship, and "They are so lesbian here." And as a girl, the funny thing is, as a girl you are like "No they're not" but at the same time we're also like "BUT THESE TWO BOYS!!! I'm sure they're ..."

Dora: And the worst part is that maybe they're [the male K-pop fans] doing the same.

Bitten: The worst part is that boys, all the boys looking at K-pop from the outside are saying, "Yes, damn they are all homosexual."

Dora: It was so funny that once there was a rumor that Baekhyun [from EXO] is dating Taeyeon [from Girls' Generation]. And then followed: "He is straight? What if they are all straight!!"

Bitten: It was so funny because no one had considered that. "It is possible ... it is possible that they're not all gay!!!"

Dora: What's going on ...

Bitten: It hadn't occurred to people. What if the others also weren't homosexual? What do we do? It is of course all chaos for those who've written fan fiction and slash with them. It is kinda like 'What do I do now? I've written long 200.000 word novels about these two persons. I've spent all my hours and the night on this.' It was the same thing ... There was a very very big couple from SHINee called Jongkey [Jonghyun and Key]. They are also very big, very recognized in K-pop but then it was made public that Jonghyun had a girlfriend. And all of a sudden there was an outcry, right, because all the girls were just like 'I was totally sure he was homosexual.' And it happens every time. I simply believe there are people who just delete their hard drive.

Fan fiction

Interview with Camilla

Bitten and Dora had first pointed me towards their friend Camilla, whom they described as an avid reader of fan fiction as well as a writer of stories herself. I first discussed this with Camilla in a joint interview with Dora and, finally, on July 15, 2015, I interviewed her about fan fiction and her mind-writing. (See also *Part One: Camilla – ubiquity and mind-writing* pp. 35-37). This section also excerpts three fan fictions by Mathilde, Caroline and Ida.

Martin: What I'm trying to understand is how Korean pop culture inspires fans to create all kinds of things – cover dance, fanfic, blogs and so forth. Your fanfic may fit into that context. So are you inspired by plots and character dynamics in K-dramas? Or is it more anime, manga and everyday life situations?

Camilla: With K-pop I actually have a story in my mind. The characters are indeed from anime, and they are then living like 'K-pop idols'. But with

K-pop I actually get a lot of inspiration from the interviews or shows they are doing in which you experience their friendship and comradeship.

Martin: So you create a hybrid of K-pop and anime in which the anime characters are imagined and written into the K-pop universe, and in which plot, mood and character dynamics are built up around the friendship and comradeship of the K-pop artists?

Camilla: That's exactly what it is. Or at least I have a story like that, but often I take the dynamics and friendships between different K-pop idols and use them in other contexts

Martin: I know you said that you are mind-writing your fanfics but have you in fact also read other fanfic writers who are working on anime and K-pop artists in the same way as you do?

Camilla: Personally, I don't know anyone doing that but I know that some fanfic writers do that. I have come across a few fanfics which are exactly about anime characters in the K-pop universe.

Martin: The story, which you are mind-writing on, is it based upon a particular anime and then on many different K-pop artists in a lot of different shows and interviews? Or is it based upon K-pop artists from a single group?

Camilla: It is a story with characters, protagonists from an anime called *Beyblade*. And then it is about the whole process from rookie to top idol in the K-pop universe. And then it is based upon a lot of K-pop idols and the stuff that they have experienced, the things they are doing and the way they are living.

Martin: *Beyblade*. You mentioned that anime several times when we talked. [You said it was] your first anime favourite which got you into reading fanfic. When for example you see an interview with an idol, then you 'think it into' an episode of your *Beyblade* fanfic ... is it something along those lines? And in that way your fanfic is in constant development as you time and again can return to the surely many episodes that you have in mind and re-write them?

Camilla: Something like that. I would probably not so much use what he/the idol said, but maybe more so the situation. If for example during a show he told an embarrassing story which happened to him and another member of the group, then I would take that situation and maybe make up my own embarrassing story, which would better fit the characters and maybe the rest of the story. But yes, that story and many others are in constant development and since I do not write them down, they can be remade constantly and developed.

Nu'est Fan Fiction

Nu'est was a minor band from a minor agency, and not many knew them. But I did! I was a huge fan. Their music along with other K-pop bands has helped me through difficult times. It has been my place to escape to. Since then, they have had their breakthrough and attained success much to the delight of me and other fans! I wrote the story about JR and Ren (their artist names) because I felt they were so cute together. But surely it is pure fiction and is completely unrelated to them as persons. The narrator is my fictive version of JR who falls headlong in love at first sight with Ren (something I believe everyone would do).

Mathilde, February 9, 2019.

Mathilde / Perfect

It was just another Friday night; the boys and I were walking to the bar as usual, when suddenly he was there. Eyes downcast, hair concealing his face, walking without watching where he was going.

Minhyun was talking animatedly to Aron, and walked directly into him, making them both stumble. "Oh fuck, sorry!" Minhyun exclaimed, and we all stopped and looked at the newcomer, who revealed his face at that moment.

And I was gone. Because fuck if he wasn't the cutest guy I had ever seen.

"I-It's okay, I-I was l-looking at the g-ground, it was st-stupid, I-I..." He looked nervous; as if he was afraid we would hurt him or something. "Hey, it's okay! Are you alright?" He just nodded and looked back down. "Hey, someone like you shouldn't walk around alone at night!" Aron said with a hint of mischief, eyeing the boy's delicate features. His hands clenched as he stared back at Aron with venom in his eyes and replied "Could say the same about you, dickhead!" And for the first time ever I saw Aron speechless. The guy looked scared, like he regretted his outbreak, but then Aron laughed out loud and swung an arm around the pretty boy's shoulder whilst saying "I like you! We're going to The Utopian, wanna join?" The pretty one smiled and said that yes, he would love to, and introductions were made while I was still in awe. His looks and attitude combined, I thought this might be an evil prank from faith, because this one was too fucking perfect. Something had to go wrong.

I came to my senses as Aron's introduction round reached me: "and this is our fairy-prince, Junior Royal!" I punched him in the arm that wasn't wrapped around the beauty as I retorted "and this is our dickhead, Aron, but you already pointed that out!" "Ouch man! Jeez, you keep forgetting that you have huge muscles now!" "No, you keep forgetting I have huge muscles now" I laughed as he skulked. "I'm Ren" the pretty one said, and chuckled at our confused expressions. "What kind of name is that?" Baekho asked. "My name" he cheekily replied, and if I hadn't liked him before, I definitely would have around now. "So anyway, do you reeeally think that Sohee would like that? I really need an honest answer guys!" Minhyun continued the previous conversation as if nothing had happened, while we began walking to the bar again. The others answered like before, that he knew her best, and they really had no idea, while I totally casually and smoothly slit up on the other side of Ren and asked "soooo where were you going?" He sent me a cute timid smile and said "I don't really know, I just walked."

While inwardly scolding myself because this guy was way out of my league and probably straight as well, I asked him to explain, and he said that his parents never let him go anywhere, so it was nice to just be out for once. "Lucky you ran into us then, we're the funniest people in the world! Baek, get newkid a beer, we have to show him a good time!"

Super Junior Fan Fiction

Ida / Everyday Miracles (excerpt)

(See Ida / clear borders, blurred boundaries p. 42)

Leeteuk was currently looking through the job section of the paper, sipping his coffee while tapping his pen on the block of paper he had placed to his right. As it was, his current employer had plans of marriage within the month, meaning that she would become a stay-at-home mum while her new husband would work, making a live-in nanny unnecessary. Though he had had a good time with this family, loving the two girls he had looked after, he found that he looked forward to a new challenge. There were quite a lot of ads in the job section, some more interesting than others, but one in particular caught his interest.

> Full-time nanny M/F
>
> Full-time nanny for four kids needed. Live-in position. Generous pay and good facilities at nanny's disposal such as home gym and car. Has to have previous experience. Contract for at least a year, preferably longer.

"Hmm, sounds interesting," Leeteuk mumbled to himself while scribbling down the contact information; he preferred long-term positions as it gave him a better chance to establish a relationship with the children he took care of, rather than only taking care of the children a month or two. He figured that he might as well give it a try and send an application.

"How may I help you?" A static voice filtered through the speaker system at the front gate a few seconds after Leeteuk had pressed the button. It had taken him a bit to get over the grandness of the house and gather enough courage to actually make his presence known.

"I'm here for an interview with Mr. Kim," Leeteuk informed and smiled up at where he thought the camera was, hoping that it wasn't one of those cameras that made the middle of your face larger than the rest.

"Oh, about the nanny position?" Leeteuk nodded. "Cool! Let me buzz you in!" the enthusiastic reply came and a buzzing sound was heard as the gates opened.

As Leeteuk made his way up to the house, the front door was opened, revealing a man who looked quite young. Too young to have four kids, Leeteuk thought as he studied the smiling man. His eyes had disappeared when the smile appeared on his face and his cheeks were chubby, making him look like some kind of cross between a chipmunk and a fat baby.

"Mr. Kim?" he asked as he reached his hand out in front of him to greet the male.

"Oh, no no, I am Henry, his personal assistant!" he chirped happily. "Mr. Kim just has some things he needed to finish before he is ready for the interview, so he asked me to excuse him and take you to the library to wait for him there. He has read the application you sent and checked all your papers and he seemed rather pleased, though," the man happily chatted as he began to lead Leeteuk into the huge house.

Leeteuk was a bit awestruck with the grandeur of the house, if he was being honest. Even though it was big and luxurious there was an air of emptiness over it. It didn't quite feel like a *home* and Leeteuk couldn't help but wonder how it was for the kids to grow up in an environment such as this. The house had two floors and he was led up a large staircase. He noted that there were baby gates both at the top and the bottom and smiled; this showed responsibility from the parents' side which was always a good sign. After having walked down a rather spacious hallway with doors on both sides, some open and presenting what clearly looked like children's rooms, he was led into a rather large room with bookshelves covering all three walls while the last wall was almost entirely made of glass and had a door leading out to a balcony where there was a splendid view of the garden behind the house.

"If you will just wait here, I am sure it won't be long before Kangin is done," the chipmunk-like male instructed. Leeteuk frowned in question.

"Kangin?" he asked. He was sure the name in the ad had been Kim Youngwoon unless he was very much mistaken.

"Oh, that's a nickname he has gained over the years. He can be rather ... strong when dealing with the company and such, so someone named him Kangin and that just kind of stuck with him, I guess," Henry explained, giving a half-bow before making his way out of the room and leaving Leeteuk to inspect the many books.

He had always loved to read and his secret fantasy since he was a kid had been to get a library that was like Belle's in 'Beauty and the Beast', and though this was not at all of that scale, it was still closer to his fantasy than anything else he had ever seen, outside of the one in the castle he had visited when he had been in England. He wandered around, looking at the many titles, feeling the overwhelming desire to take any one of them and go to the comfortable sofa chair that stood near the window and start reading.

However, his thoughts were soon interrupted by a loud wail, and before he had time to even think he set out to find the source of the sound. He re-entered the hallway and found a door on the other side slightly ajar, the sobbing and whimpering clearly coming from that room. He pushed the door open and was met with the sight of a chubby toddler with tears streaming down his fat cheeks. Without thinking, he hurried over to the toddler and crouched down.

"What's wrong, sweetie?" he asked in a soft voice so as not to scare the small boy. The boy stopped wailing to look at the stranger in front of him but he continued whimpering.

"Hae and Hyuk took Kiki!" the toddler sniffled with a quivering lower lip before starting all over with the wailing again. Though Leeteuk didn't know any of the said persons (or objects) he was quick to scoop the toddler up into his arms and balance him on his hip.

"Don't cry, darling," he cooed as he stroked the soft baby hair away from the toddler's face and gently dried away his tears.

"Do you want to read a book until Hae and Hyuk come back?" he asked, having noticed the small bookshelf in the corner filled with children's books. The toddler nodded warily, sniffing once before he rested his head on Leeteuk's shoulder and started sucking on his thumb. *Well, he certainly isn't afraid of strangers*, Leeteuk thought before going over to the bookshelf. "Is there a special book you want to read?" he asked and the toddler's eyes lit up.

"Weed aliphant?" he asked shyly. Leeteuk nodded and picked up the first book he spotted with an elephant on the cover. Luckily it seemed to be the one the toddler had meant as his eyes lit up in joy and he clapped his small hands together in enthusiasm. Leeteuk smiled and sat down on the floor with his back against the wall, rearranging the toddler so it was more comfortable for the both of them.

"Can you tell me your name?" Leeteuk asked since he had no idea what the toddler was called. He received a huge smile in response to the question.

"Wookie!" the boy chirped happily and snuggled closer to his new found friend. He only hoped that this friend would stay longer than the last one.

"I'm Teukie," Leeteuk introduced, unable to stop smiling at the boy's actions before turning to the first page of the book, reading aloud for the toddler.

As he made his way through the pages of the book he noticed two heads peeking into the room; he was pretty certain that these were the in-famous Hae and Hyuk Wookie had been talking about. However, he decided that it was best to let them come to him instead of scaring them by suddenly turning his attention to them. He heard them whisper to each other before they finally made an entrance. He looked up from the book at the same time as Wookie.

"Well, hello," he greeted with a friendly smile. "Who might you two be?" he asked and the boys immediately seemed to gain quite a lot of energy from the attention. They were bouncing over to the stranger and their little brother before introducing themselves.

"I'm Hae!" one of them exclaimed, a brown mop of messy hair on his head.

"And I'm Hyuk!" the other chirped with a huge gummy smile, revealing a missing front tooth.

"Oh, so you were the ones who took Kiki from Wookie?" Leeteuk said with a gentle but still stern voice. The boys suddenly looked down in shame and Hae nodded quietly.

"We just wanted to play with her," Hae said in a sad tone, fidgeting with his hands.

"Well, if you go get her and give her back to Wookie again then you can choose the next book we read, how about that?" he suggested and the boys eagerly agreed, running out of the room to get said plushie (at least Leeteuk assumed it was a plushie by now) and bring it back to their brother.

Wookie seemed content with the way things had developed, but also tired from the excitement. He yawned as he snuggled even closer to Leeteuk, trying to keep his eyes open, but he was fighting a losing battle it seemed. Leeteuk smiled at the young boy and started humming a soft tune. The toddler was soon fast asleep, one hand clutching the fabric of Leeteuk's shirt.

"Wookie seems to like you," a deep voice came from the door.

Leeteuk jumped slightly in surprise and then quickly checked that he hadn't woken up said toddler with his start before turning his attention to the door. The man standing there was tall and rather muscular. He had friendly eyes and he was smiling slightly at the sight of his son sleeping peacefully for what seemed like the first time in months. He was clad in a deep blue suit and despite his friendly demeanour he had a no-nonsense air around him. He had heard Leeteuk's dealing with the twins and seen how he acted with Wookie after the twins left.

"I'm sorry, I was going to wait in the library but he started crying and before I thought about it I was in here and talking to him to calm him down. I'm sorry," Leeteuk apologised, knowing that he might very well have overstepped some boundaries by entering the nursery before he had been introduced to the father. The taller man chuckled, shaking his head as he stepped into the room, sitting down in front of him. "We can go to the library, I, I guess I just need to tuck him in first," Leeteuk said, before making to stand up.

Kangin hurriedly stopped him, waving his arms to get him to abort the motion. "No, please sit! It's the first time in months he's been sleeping peacefully," he said, sounding worn out at the very thought. He rubbed his temples before looking Leeteuk over, analysing him. Leeteuk sat back against the wall and held the toddler tighter. The toddler remained peacefully sleeping, as if nothing had happened. "I'm Youngwoon by the way, but you can call me Kangin. So, what happened that had him crying? Was it the twins again?" he asked.

Leeteuk nodded. “Yes, apparently Hae and Hyuk took Kiki,” he replied and Kangin smiled gently to himself.

“Donghae and Hyukjae,” he informed with a smile. “And this little guy is Ryeowook although we all call him Wookie,” he said as he nodded towards the toddler. “Siwon is probably reading somewhere. He is the oldest. He is eight,” he continued and Leeteuk couldn't help but smile at the weird situation. He had never been interviewed for a job before while sitting on the floor with a sleeping toddler on his front. The house seemed to be nothing like the family; the family reflected a lot more warmth.

EXO / SHINee Fan Fiction

I worked on “Between Braids and Kisses” from 2013 to 2015. The story is based on the two K-pop groups SHINee and EXO, mainly inspired by EXO's “WOLF”-era, which was the era that brought me into the interest of said K-pop group. The main characters in the story is Lee Taemin, the main dancer from SHINee, and Kai, the main dancer from EXO. Taemin is a spoiled rich kid, battling with social anxiety and a suppressed sexuality, while Kai is the leader of a gang consisting of the rest of the EXO members. Despite their obvious differences, the two of them fall in love, even though it turns out that they had actually known each other for longer than they had thought, as Kai is a childhood friend that moved away from Taemin's neighbourhood when they were barely teenagers. I chose to write about these two K-pop idols as they're really close friends, and even look alike quite a bit. They knew each other during their trainee days and seem to have a very close bromance bond that I really adore.

Caroline, February 15, 2019.

Caroline / Between Braids and Kisses

Chapter 1: All About You (excerpt)

Taemin took a deep breath as he walked out of the school gates on his way to freedom after just another boring day at school with all the usual people and bullies to bug him. He had to walk out of the back entrance of the school, because he was pretty sure that the bullies were waiting for him at the main entrance. And oh how was he right.

Yeah, his life sucked. He couldn't go one day without people yelling stuff after him, calling him things he didn't even like thinking about, but let's just say that everyone at the school knew that he was gay. Being gay and shy isn't a good combination, because Taemin never dared to protest, he was always scared of being beaten by the stronger guys – again. So he just accepted their insulting words and only cried in secret, only at home.

His mom would always worry about him when he got home with new bruises, maybe even with his own bloodstains on his school uniform. His dad, on the other hand, didn't care much about him, since he found out about his sexuality. He barely looked at him when the five of them ate dinner together. He never said goodbye to him when Taemin left for school. It was like a family that was about to part.

Taemin's parents didn't really accept that their son liked guys, they just hoped that their son would some day fall for a girl.

Like that was gonna happen.

Taemin crossed the corner of the school fence and could already then see the usual path that he had to take to get home. He had to pass the street where gangs usually hung out. Where there were drug dealers in the alloyways, trying to talk him into buying some, or maybe even try a little bit for free.

He couldn't wait to get his driver's license, and then he wouldn't have to listen to all those damn gangs, drug dealers and fights, they were all even worse than his schoolmates, even though they had never beaten him up. Oh, and Taemin hated the smell of hash. It was everywhere. It smelled like spruce.

Taemin bit his lower lip as he was now walking on the sidewalk to one of the larger, grey apartments, which looked like it could crumble any second. There was cracks meters up the walls of the building, which were covered well with all the colourful graffiti, which he admitted that he sometimes liked, but it depended on how it looked, of course. If it was those, boring, simple letters, only painted with black and white paint just to show that '*I was here*' or something, he disliked it. But if it was those beautiful, big paintings of all kinds of things, he loved it.

He especially liked those big graffiti paintings of wolves, they were everywhere in this neighborhood.

Paintings of big, grey or black wolves that howled at the shining full moon, with the beautiful, deep night sky as the background, with hundreds of stars on it, and maybe a few dark clouds here and there. They were usually painted on the naked walls of the tall apartment buildings.

It could really impress him, he loved that kind of art.

"Hey! What are you doing here?!" Taemin suddenly gasped as he saw a few guys, a bit older than him, yelling at him a few meters away, coming closer. They were wearing black and white clothes, baggy pants and tank tops or hoodies and had bandanas around their heads.

He already knew who they were, and he didn't want any trouble with them.

Their hands were holding a few spraying cans in all kinds of colours, and Taemin quickly turned away from the beautiful graffiti painting and kept walking, walking past them and continued on his way home.

"That's right! Keep walking!" they yelled again, and Taemin just bit his lower lip harder this time. He could still hear them laugh far behind him. He hated those people, every single one of them. But he didn't wanna cry, not again. Last time he cried in front of those people, they just started laughing louder, and he was pretty sure that it was the reason why they always bugged him now.

They wanted to make him cry, they tried to make him cry.

"I'll show them … When they're rotting in jail in a few years, I'll be on top of the world," he mumbled for himself, referring to the big company that his father owned.

"Yo, Kai!"

Those two words were the only words Taemin needed to freeze completely. He hesitated before he turned his head to look in the direction of the words. It was the usual place, in the backyard of the apartment building with the graffiti.

There were about fifteen guys, and a few girls, all in black and white outfits – mostly black, with the same bandanas as the guys who were yelling at Taemin a few minutes ago.

"Do you have the goods?" the deep voice that made Taemin's heart flutter asked his gang member. Taemin's eyes traveled from the gang member to Kai, who was sitting on top of a few crates, with a skinny girl with not much clothes on by his side. Kai was a beautiful guy, when he didn't have a cigarette or such between his plump lips. His skin was slightly tanned, which just made him even sexier in Taemin's eyes, especially the fact that even though Kai was thin he wasn't skinny – his arms had a hint of muscles, and Taemin was pretty sure that so did his stomach. He really wanted so find out, so badly. Kai's hair was dark, almost black, styled in cornrows and long, fake braids, which Taemin didn't know whether he liked or not.

Oh God, why did he have to like Kai, of all people?!

Cover dance

During my conversations with Dora, she frequently mentioned cover dance activities as one of the ways in which she was active as a fan of K-pop. Occasionally, she made cover dance videos with Bitten as video photographer and editor. These videos they posted on their YouTube channels. Dora also made a cover dance of 'Pretty Age 25' by Song Ji Eun at the National Museum of Denmark K-Day event in 2016. This section focuses on a key element in Dora's cover dance, namely *aegyo*, which the below interview excerpt revolves around. The cover dance is documented through still photos from two cover dance videos.

Martin: What is *aegyo* to you?

Dora: Even though I know the correct meaning of the word, which is 'cute' if one were to translate it from Korean into Danish, it is a certain kind of 'cuteness'. When I hear the word aegyo, I think about a Korean girl or young woman with large eyes, a light or bright make-up, bright and peach coloured lips, who looks innocent. However, it is not only referring to Korean and Asian women. People with an interest in Korea or K-pop may also go for the "aegyo" style – which some people here [in Denmark] maybe will see as "girlish" – as aegyo is often seen in music videos made both for boy groups and girl groups. These fans of Korea and K-pop will often wear the light make-up, skirt, stockings and a colourful blouse. They may also wear "childish" accessories such as earrings that look like ice cream cones or a huge plastic heart, which hangs from a necklace. However, the accessories are not a must to attain the style. There may also be animal motifs such as tights where it looks like one is wearing stockings, where the top part of the stocking looks like a bear, a cat, Totoro [a Japanese animation character] or something else. I should probably say that there are other ways to attain this look, and that this is just one example. I may also come up with a look which indicates aegyo.

In everyday language I do not use the word very often as not everyone knows the meaning of the word, but among my friends interested in Korea and K-pop the word may come out of my mouth once in a while. Often it will follow the Danish meaning as for example "Ohhh you're so cute. So *aegyo*". The word may also occur if I have to describe a music video and/or which style the band in the music video has. For example, "They are *aegyo*" or "It is a bit too much *aegyo* for me." "They are acting out far too much *aegyo* for me to take it seriously."

Martin: Where do you see *aegyo* in the dances that you are doing covers of?

Dora: A sign that a dance has *aegyo* is that it is more aiming for charm than trying to impress the spectators with the steps themselves. Focus is more on the face, the steps are easy and flowing. Often there is a playfulness in the dance and there may occur a pause in which there is no special step but it is all about looking cute, which often is shown by looking surprised, waving at the audience and such.

There are steps in the dance which consist of pointing at the face, hide behind the hands and "appear" or simply having the hands close to the face so as to get the focus of the spectators up to the face. The face often also has a bigger significance in a dance where *aegyo* is present. For example, the head is turned from side to side or it is jerked from side to side. This whole focus on the face/head is an aid so as to charm the spectators.

Martin: How do you work on expressing aegyo in your cover dance?

Dora: I put a lot of focus on being charming. There is a light smile on my lips, my facial expressions are often changed throughout the dance. For example, I may turn one side of my face out towards the "spectators" and smile, and next I turn the other side out with a surprised expression. I only do this, however, if it fits into my dance.

I try to make it look like the dance is a game that I'm playing and as something which is more natural, a part of me. If I am shooting a video of the dance I also consider which clothes I am wearing. Like, in many of my other covers I study what they are wearing in the music video and their style and try to find something which resembles it as much as possible. This clothing more or less is made up of the style I explained in your first question.

I also focus on the make-up. I make sure that it is light and bright. Preferably, it should accentuate my eyes but without wearing a heavy or dark eyeshadow. *Aegyo* inspired make-up often tries to go towards the natural look.

Fan art

Pernille participated in the National Museum of Denmark K-Day (2015) where she organized a fan room – an improvised exhibition of fan accessories and objects. Later, I came across her social media profile where she posted her fan art. At the outset, I was interested in collecting two pieces of her fan art made on the pages of a Danish book. I realized, however, that Pernille had gifted them to her friends Sara and Lene. Instead, we agreed that I could collect scanned copies of her fan art.

The following is a series of excerpts from my conversation with Pernille, Lene and Sara about fan art involving Thunder from MBLAQ and Jonghyun from SHINee. As the conversation evolved, I realized that not only fan art but also stories are made and shared among these three friends. This section, then, includes examples of Pernille's fan art, as well as excerpts of the stories that the three friends shared about Thunder and Jonghyun.

Pernille Talking about Her Fan Art

Pernille: I had been going through a period of thinking: "I don't know how to draw. I don't know how to paint. Ah, it's such a long time since I have done anything." And then I decided that I would just make something. And then I wanted to make something for her [Lene's] birthday, which I could send to her. And I had bought this old book, which I had hollowed out and then I had taken some of the pages out. It was this book about entertainment in Copenhagen during the 1880's. And then I was painting it while I was talking to her [Lene] on Skype, while trying to make sure that she didn't see that I was sitting with painting brushes and all of that.

Martin: What was it that caught your attention about this book? Was it the expression in it? The colour? Or was it the stories?

Pernille: I mean, the reason why I bought it was because it was tiny and thick. And then I could hollow it out and put things inside it.

Martin: Okay. So you actually saw it, when you bought it, as something you could use for something else?

Pernille: Exactly. Yeah, I was looking for a book that I could hollow out. So that's why I bought it. Then I had taken out some of the pages because after I had glued the pages together it was too big. Then I had to take out some of the pages. And then I found a page where there was some space between [the lines] ... so that his eye could fit in there. I just took, yeah, a page where ... You can also see it here; where there is no text in the eye. And then I drew. Then I found a nice picture of Jonghyun and painted him.

Martin: And what made you want to combine this book that talks about Copenhagen in the old days and these drawings here? Is it something you have done before, this kind of expression?

Pernille: Not really. I think I chose the book pages specifically because of their yellowish colour. And then I didn't have to make the skin colour. I just had to make the highlights and the shadows on them. So it was kind of like cutting corners. Or something like that. Or to make it easier. And also because I had been thinking that I didn't know how to draw, so I had to simplify the painting technique. And I thought, I can just use this because it's a nice yellowish colour, which could pass as a skin colour. Or something see-through. I just think that that was the main reason why I picked those pages.

Martin: And the result of having the text is also quite interesting, I think.

Pernille: Agreed. I think that I have seen others painting on old newspapers and such. So I think I got the idea from there.

Martin: How many have you made in total of these?

Pernille: I have only made these two here. And then I actually have one that's half done at home.

Martin: Two and a half?

Pernille: Two and a half. Because I made this one as a birthday present. There was this other time where I had done some other drawings, which I had gifted as Christmas presents to all my friends. And I thought that this could be the birthday presents that year. And it was in 2015 – it's in '15 that I painted those two. I started with Thunder. And then I actually also found pictures for my two other friends and for myself as well. I wanted to paint them but I never did.

Martin: But did you decide yourself that it had to be these two? Or was it kind of in dialogue?

Pernille: The reason why I chose those characters was because, ever since we started with K-pop we had established our own bias, our favourite, in all the groups we were listening to. It was kind of like I had to make their ultimate bias.

Martin: So you weren't really unsure about who it had to be?

Pernille: Not at all. I think that after I drew Jonghyun, then I think I wrote you

[Sara] to ask if Thunder with pink hair was still your favourite. And it was. And I found a picture of him with pink hair.

Martin: Is it taken directly from a photograph? Or is this how you imagine him? Or is it from other fan art? I mean the portrait, where did you get the portrait from?

Pernille: I mean, I just goggled it. I specifically think that Jonghyun's picture was something that was relatively newly published. It was from some photo shoot where he had this grey hair, which sometimes looked grey, sometimes green, sometimes blue. So we talked a lot about his hair colour at that time. And it was just a really nice picture. And the same for ... ah ... right now I don't remember where Thunder's picture is from. I probably still have it on my computer; the original.

Martin: But both are based on photos of them?

Pernille: Yeah. I mean, I had the picture on the phone or on the computer, and then I made a sketch and then painted them afterwards.

Martin: Is it the first time that you paint for your girlfriends? Painting biases? Or is it something you have done before in other media?

Pernille: Years back I drew some black-and-white pencil drawings. Which I don't think are particularly nice anymore, just because I have gotten better.

Lene: I still like them.

Pernille: Back then I combined pictures of the girls and [their] biases. And then I put them together so that they [their biases] kiss them [Lene and Sara] on the forehead or something like that.

Martin: The same two biases?

Pernille: The same! Yeah, we have been pretty consistent with them. And I have also drawn ... we have this idea that each bias has an animal, which is based on some variety shows and such. And I have drawn those animals once, also in watercolour, for each of you guys.

Martin: Okay, so they exist in several kinds of expressions and as animals and mixed together?

Pernille: Exactly.

Martin: It's very interesting that this is actually just one example of what you have done.

Pernille: Yes, exactly. I have been using it as an excuse that I'm creative … I need to make something creative. What tools do I have that I can draw with and for others? And I sold a couple of them, but then stopped because it was too troublesome to … I don't feel good about getting rid of my drawings unless it's for my girlfriends who hang them on their wall, and who enjoy them, so that I get to see them [the drawings] once in a while.

Martin: So they still mean something to you?

Pernille: I mean, they do because all of us have been talking mainly about these two groups for many years [MBLAQ and SHINee]. So in that way they also mean something to me because I like those two groups. I draw for myself and for my girlfriends.

Martin: It kind of stays in the family in a way.

Pernille: Yeah, exactly! It kind of does.

Lene: Then you can still keep an eye on them in that case.

Pernille: Yeah, like check every time I visit: "Yes, they are still up on the wall. Good! That's important!"

Sara Talking about Fan Art portraying Thunder from Mblaq

Sara: The first time I saw the group [MBLAQ] I thought that he [Thunder] was the ugliest one. Actually I didn't like him. And then one day I just think that I was sitting in front of my computer and was watching something featuring him. And then all of the sudden my brain and body was like:

Thunder

Jonghyun

"He's your favourite." And ever since that he has just been my number one.

Lene: You just know.

Pernille: It just hits you!

Martin: Was it the way he sang? Or was it his appearance?

Sara: It was just everything.

Martin: Is it completely wrong to compare it to being in love?

Sara: It is [like being in love]. It's some of the same feelings you get. Like falling in love with someone.

Pernille: It's very strange because it's people on a screen. But yeah, that's how it is.

Lene: Yeah, because you also feel like it's silly. That you can like someone who you don't know. It's kind of strange.

Pernille: I like to think of it as "it's the idea of that person." Because maybe if you meet them face to face they might prove to be total jerks. We can't know that for sure.

Martin: Where is he [Thunder]? Where do you have this drawing?

Sara: I mean, it's on my wall. I have a wall at home. I have this two-metre-long desk, and above the desk I have different Thunder things ... And in the hallway, on my fridge, I also have some pictures of him.

Martin: He is in a lot of places.

Sara: Everywhere!

Lene Talking about Fan Art portraying Jonghyun from Shinee

Martin: He [Jonghyun] is a bit more famous [than Thunder].

Lene: Yeah, he is. Which is kind of annoying when you are a fan. I mean, the good thing about him was that there was way more stuff with him.

Martin: And when did he become your bias?

Lene: First time I watched a K-pop music video, that was SHINee. And I don't know why. I saw him and thought "Jeez, that is some ugly hair!" That's how it started.

Martin: Something is repeating itself here! Something keeps coming up! [There's something about something starting off as ugly in a way.]

Lene: It's also just in general, [to watch] Asian things when you are used to watching Danish. And then he had this spiky hair. It wasn't pretty.

Martin: So at that time you weren't really interested in K-pop?

Lene: Not at all! I hadn't even heard ... I think I had heard one song before that and it just hadn't caught my interest. But then when I heard their song I think it was the only song I listened to that day. I think it was because I was able to recognize him that I thought "Well, I like him." And I was able to recognize his voice. And then I just started to listen to his stuff.

Martin: So actually, your interest in Korea, or at least in K-pop and your bias here, those two things are totally connected in a way.

Lene: Yeah, actually they are. Because it was their song that made it happen. And it was because I kept looking at him. And I was able to recognize him.

Martin: And how long did it take from you entered K-pop and watched this video till you thought "This is my bias"? I mean, this type of fan language; do you remember when he went from being the guy with the ugly hair to the guy with the ugly hair, who is my bias?

Lene: I didn't know that it was called a bias at the time. But I think from when I watched it actually. I mean, like maybe a week after or something like that. But I had to learn the language first of course.

Martin: If you had to describe him to a new K-pop fan, who didn't know him. How would you describe him?

Lene: Creative. Talented. And sensitive. Very sensitive, I think. I mean, every time he did some concert without his [fellow] members, then he would write them all the time and he brought them together and he was very bad at being without them. So he was very sensitive and ... I think, very like, he needed comfort. But yes, creative at least. And a good song writer. And singer of course.

Martin: Do you do the same as [Sara] ... You were explaining how you have ... what was it? In front of the desk and in the hallway ...

Lene: Everywhere.

Martin: Everywhere. Is yours the same?

Lene: It used to be. My room before I moved, all the walls were ... Back then it was. But not anymore. Because right now I don't like to look at him [Jonghyun tragically passed away on December 17, 2017]. So after that, no. But not even before that, but that was because we just moved a couple of months before that. Then I hadn't managed to put something up. So now I have a small figurine of him on display. At the moment, that's all.

Sara, Lene and Pernille about sharing Stories

Sara: There was this extended period of time where we had no inhibitions ... then we wrote these short fan fictions and sent them to each other. A bit like she [Pernille] made fan art secretly then, me and Lene, we have written secret fan fictions. And then we sent them ...

Pernille: Just like these small ones in text messages.

Sara: Short ones in a text message.

Martin: Kind of short everyday stories?

Sara: Yes.

Martin: What could it be, a story like that? What could it be for example?

Sara: I mean, it's just like these cute stories where it's kind of ...

Lene: A date or something like that.

Pernille: Small scenarios.

Sara: Yeah, these small scenarios where you are on a date together [with your bias] or you are at home cooking or something like that. Everyday stuff.

Lene: I think so too. Those short ones. I liked that.

Pernille: Then there was a time where you would wake up to a message and [be like] "Ah! Hi!"

Martin: I have never heard about this before! I mean, I know about fan fiction. As these long stories on Asianfanfics and so on. But also as stories you write to each other?

Lene: At one point we used to do it a lot, where you would text people at night so that when they wake up then ...

Sara: Then they had like a "Good morning!"

Lene: Like a morning story.

Pernille: But it was just something down the lines of "Imagine that you wake up next to [him] and he is snoring" or something like that.

Martin: But would you then write about your bias or your friends' biases?

Pernille: If I had to write to those two, then I would write about them and their biases.

Sara: And then it would often be as a 1st person narrator. Or as, so that you wrote, like, as if you were the person yourself together with their bias.

Martin: That also says something about just how close you are to each other. Because you have to be able to, if the stories are to be good, you have to be able to completely identify yourself with this "I," which you are writing about, right?

Lene: And we talked a lot, I mean ... we still talk about K-pop, but we talked a lot about it in the beginning. On top of that, we are just really good friends.

> "Jonghyun wrapped his arms calmingly around you, as you snuggled into his chest. He gently kissed your forehead, and even though you weren't tired before, you quickly fell asleep in his embrace."

"ONCE UPON A TIME…"
"…AND THEN!"

"You were listening to music as you walked, not paying much attention to your surroundings. Suddenly two arms wrapped around your waist. You got startled, as you hadn't noticed anyone, when you heard Joon say "Hey aegi" [kid], as he pulled you into an embrace and placed his head on your shoulder."

Sara: And then there's some of them [the fan fictions] where we have been sitting together, talking about some scenarios between our biases and then I went home and wrote them down.

Martin: Okay, I see. So that's also something you do? I mean, make scenarios about your biases together?

Sara: Yeah.

Martin: Where it's not this 1st person narrator, but then these two biases?

Sara: Yeah, as the main part where we aren't actually a part of the story.

Martin: Okay, I see. So it's actually a completely different type of story then.

Sara: Where they ... how they interact with each other.

Martin: What's the content of a story like that, for example?

Sara: I mean, for example it could be about how SHINee and MBLAQ, how they actually became friends. And then we have seen some clips of how, for example, a guy named Joon and Onew were friends in real life. And then we made up how the others [group members] were supposed to then befriend each other.

Martin: So you build on top of these stories that are already out there somewhere?

Sara: Yeah. How they would be together in their world.

Conclusion

This volume began with the juxtaposition of my own road towards Korea in 1993 with the plural, mediated and inter-personal ways in which a young Danish woman moves through Korean terrain in her everyday life in Copenhagen in 2015. I have coined the term 'K-pop reality' to describe the experience of moving through this terrain. This K-pop reality is not only being formed by Korean aesthetics and visuals, storytelling and ideals. A main focus in this book has been the creative ways that these Danish fans are productively engaged in forming and formatting this 'K-pop reality'. Part of the existing literature has a tendency to strive to understand how East Asian popular culture, not least contents made by the creative industries of Japan and Korea, partake in shaping and forming an inter-Asian modernity, a shared sociality across Asia. At the same time, the 'Western' fan of Asian popular culture is sometimes considered from the perspective of 'cultural appropriation'. While, surely, there may be gendered and cultural imbalances at play in the ways young Danish women think, talk about, express and act upon their fannish desires for Korean male performers and their 'flawlessly flawed masculinities', it is my main ambition with this book to consider these Danish producer-consumers in the context of trans-Asian mediated referencing, and as participants in the social worlds created around East Asian popular culture.

List of Illustrations